heartless

episodes 1-3

ALWAYS A GIFT

Little Free Library

NEVER FOR SALE

USA Today Bestselling Author

J. STERLING

Edited and Interior Designed by:

Jovana Shirley

www.unforeseenediting.com

Cover Design by:

Michelle Preast

www.facebook.com/IndieBookCovers

ISBN-13: 978-1502936004
ISBN-10: 1502936003

CONTENTS

Episode 1

Episode 2

Episode 3

heartless

episode 1

PROLOGUE
Elizabeth

I walked across the busy intersection, leaving my sprawling college campus behind me, as I headed the four blocks toward my two-bedroom apartment. My school wasn't in the best area of Los Angeles, so instead of walking with my head down and eyes plastered on my cell phone screen, I pocketed my phone and looked around at my surroundings. Little did I know that the personal violation headed for me would come from within the safety of my apartment walls and not the big, bad world around me.

Keeping my pace quick, I longed to get out of the heat and into the comfort of my almost constantly running air-conditioning. Indian summers in Southern California varied between two temperatures—hot and sweltering. Today was the perfect example of the latter. When the depressingly gray stucco building appeared in the distance, I had to stop myself from running to the front door.

I had no idea what I was about to walk into would change my life dramatically.

Wait for it.

3…

2…

1…

Turning the handle, I flung the front door open and habitually went to throw my bag on the kitchen table, but something stopped me mid-toss. My roommate, Kim's, hot-pink panties dangled from her left foot as her toes curled and uncurled. Her black skirt had been pushed up as high as it would go on her waist, and it bunched up all thick in places, the fabric looking lumpy and uncomfortable. One of her hands dug into the kitchen table we shared, and I couldn't help but notice the way her pink nail polish had chipped. It looked tacky. It was funny—the stupid details that would stick in your mind when your world was about to fall apart.

Kim moaned, her voice dragging out *his* name, "Ben...oh God, Ben."

Ben.

My Ben?

My boyfriend, Ben?

Ben's head was partially blocked by Kim's thigh, but I'd know that head anywhere. Thick dark curls sat atop a lean but defined swimmer's body—a body I knew by heart after almost three years of dating exclusively.

Well, at least I had been exclusive.

My stomach lurched and twisted, and my head felt like it might roll right off my shoulders if I tilted it too much to one side. I needed to brace myself on something, but the kitchen table was the closest thing to me, and I vowed never to touch that piece of furniture ever again. Taking two steps back, I leaned against the front door, the weight of my body slamming it shut.

Ben pulled his head out from between Kim's legs and stared at me with something in his eyes. It wasn't guilt. Horror maybe?

"Elizabeth, this isn't what it looks like!" He stumbled over his words.

All I could stare at was his glistening face.

Kim screamed, attempted to push her clunky skirt down, and swatted at Ben's head as if he had attacked her without her knowledge, as if he were in the wrong. She didn't even look at me before running into her bedroom and flinging her door closed.

"It's not what it looks like," he repeated, taking a cautious step toward me.

"Don't fucking touch me." I sucked in a breath and moved away from the confinement of the door, not liking the way I felt stuck against it.

"Just hear me out." He raised his hands in the air in a gesture of surrender.

"What is there to hear out? Let me guess…" I paused, begging the sickness rising in my stomach to please keep at bay. "She tripped, and her vagina fell on your face?"

"You're such a bitch," he spit.

I took two steps back, not wanting a single iota of his body or fluids to touch me, as my jaw dropped with his accusation. "I'm a bitch? I'M A BITCH?" I shouted at him as anger rolled off me in violent waves. "You're the one cheating on me with my fucking roommate, but I'm the bitch?"

"You're never around. You're always working or interning or studying. You can't blame me for needing more, Elizabeth."

I guffawed at his idiocy and refused to accept the blame. "Oh, so this is my fault, right? I pushed you to fuck my roommate and whomever else you're fucking because I have a life outside of you?"

"You're too ambitious." His arms flailed wildly as he attempted to prove his point. "Everything you do is focused on your future, and your goals are so high, so fucking high."

I stopped him from speaking further, "So what? What the hell is wrong with being ambitious and having goals?"

"You're a woman!"

"Uh…" I balled my hands into fists. "Tread carefully, dipshit."

"Listen, Elizabeth, no guy wants a woman who's more successful than he is. Guys are supposed to be the breadwinners, the champions of the house, not the girl. I need someone who is going to support me and my dreams, not have lofty dreams of her own."

I started shaking my head, wondering if this was real. This had to be a fucking dream, so I pinched my arm. "Did I just walk out of the heat and into the nineteen forties? Who the hell are you right now?"

Staring into his shit-colored eyes, I wondered how this had never come up before. *How had I been so blinded to the fact that my boyfriend was a complete chauvinistic pig?*

"It's an old ideal, but it's still the way most guys think, Elizabeth. I promise you, I'm not the only one. You're going to have a hard time keeping any man with the way you are. You're too driven."

"Stop saying that like it's a bad thing!" I screamed, my head aching with each new thought that had entered.

"There's such a thing as being too ambitious, and that's what you are. No man can handle that kind of woman, and no man truly wants one in his life."

After shaking my head as if I could spill his words right back out of my ears, I narrowed my eyes and glared at him. "Really? No man or just you?"

"You're not listening to me. I'm trying to help you. Men want to be catered to, doted on, taken care of, and needed. You don't need anyone."

Why was that a bad thing? "I sure as shit don't need you," I agreed.

"And that's the problem. Good luck with your life. You'll *need* that at least." He shrugged with a disgusted smirk spreading across his still glossy lips.

"Get the fuck out of my apartment before I do something I might regret, like shove you down the stairs." I moved toward the front door and opened it before waving him along. When his movements stalled, I shouted, "Leave! Now! Get out!"

He did, but not before turning around and delivering one last blow. "You're heartless, you know that? It's like you don't even care."

I laughed at the irony of his words as I clearly felt my heart breaking into irreparable pieces.

Elizabeth

Eight Years Later

"Tell me why I'm going to this stupid mixer again." I peeked out from behind my office door and groaned at my overly busty assistant, Barbara.

No matter what she wore to work each day, nothing could hide those double Ds from attempting to spill out. I respected her for trying though.

Shaking her gorgeous head of dark hair, she turned to me and answered, "Because you're successful, and they invited you."

Barbara was sassy and smart—two of the reasons I'd hired her to be my assistant in the first place. I needed a strong woman who wouldn't be intimidated by or scared of me. And trust me, those qualities in a fellow female were hard to come by, especially when you were this young; and the boss. Which I was.

Barbara had been with me for over two years now, and we'd built an honest friendship around our working one. I couldn't be more thankful to have someone like her on my side. Being that I didn't have much time for a social life outside of work, I was extra grateful for her.

And I trusted her, which spoke volumes. In an industry where it was hard to count on pretty much anyone, I counted on her. I knew implicitly that she wouldn't throw me under the bus to get ahead. Barbara was what we in the business liked to call *a lifer*. She wanted to be an executive assistant, and she had no aspirations to climb the corporate ladder any higher, which was good news for me.

Barbara loved working for me, and I loved having her here. My office life would seem to fall completely the fuck apart whenever she wasn't around. That was a sign of a truly great assistant—realizing my workdays wouldn't really work without her.

I rolled my eyes. "Ugh. You know how much I hate these things." I ran my fingers through my dirty-blonde hair and pulled pieces of it across my face before letting it go and repeating the gesture. It was an old habit I'd never grown out of.

"Maybe you'll meet someone," she teased, wiggling her eyebrows at me.

"Oh, yeah, that's exactly what I need—a man in my life." I paused as I glanced down toward the floor. "No, thank you. This studio has more than enough testosterone for me."

"Well, in case you change your mind, I put together profiles of everyone who will be in attendance tonight. Nothing major, just headshots and company information, so you can make your speech more personal to the group," she said with a smile.

"I don't deserve you." I shook my head, grateful for her proactive ways.

With a wave of her hand, she giggled. "Just go and pretend you're honored to be there."

"Oh, I'm honored all right," I said with mocked enthusiasm.

She flipped through the pages in her hands. "Daniel Alexander looks hot. Make sure you talk to him."

I choked out a laugh. "Daniel Alexander, huh? Gotta love a guy with two first names."

"Don't hate. Procreate. He could have two heads for all I care—as long as they both look like this one."

She shoved a picture of him in front of my face, and even I had to admit that the guy was gorgeous. His dark hair looked perfectly styled, and I could tell that his eyes were light in color, even in the black-and-white photo. Stubble lined his chiseled chin. If I had a type anymore, which I wasn't certain that I did, this guy would be it.

"I should just send you in my place. Then, you could talk to this guy all night long."

"Don't think I haven't thought about it," she sassed.

I turned back into my office and groaned inwardly before sitting back down at my desk.

I clicked on my calendar for the day and noted the large chunk of time blocked out for the Top Thirty Under Thirty mixer later that evening. *Could they really not come up with a better, more creative name for this thing?* It sounded like a countdown show.

Being the youngest development executive in the history of the movie studio where I worked came with a lot of additional events I was required to attend. Apparently, my age and title were a big deal, but I honestly didn't care—no, scratch that. I absolutely fucking cared, but it wasn't in the same way that other people seemed to.

They only cared about my age and my gender. Rarely would my name be brought up in conversation without those two aspects being mentioned close behind. It was as if that was all that truly mattered or all that I was. I realized this was a male-dominated industry and that my company had been run by men since its inception over seventy-five years ago. So, what happened with me seemed to be on the rare side, but the truth was, women had been making a name for themselves for years now, and I wanted to be one of them. I didn't want to be known as the youngest female of anything. I wanted to be known as the best.

"Your driver will be here in thirty minutes. There's a traffic accident on the four-oh-five, so you should advise him to take the one-seventy instead and get off on Sherman."

I looked up to see my assistant's face as she placed a large manila envelope in front of me.

"Could you be more awesome?"

"Probably not. The company jet is fueled and prepped at Van Nuys. You fly into SFO and back again at your leisure. Just call the car and let them know when you've taken off. They will be waiting for you when you land. I'll see you bright and early in the morning unless,"—she paused—"Heaven forbid, you have any fun, and I don't know maybe skip your return flight."

"Oh, you'd love that, wouldn't you?" I shuffled through the loose papers on my desk, trying to coherently organize them. "You just want a day off."

"Are you kidding me? If you didn't show up, I'd have to reschedule every single meeting you have tomorrow, and those took me at least two months to schedule in the first place. So, please, Elizabeth, don't show up because you know how much I love doing the same work twice."

"You're a brat."

"I know, but I'm your brat. Have fun. Tell Daniel I said hi." She blew me a kiss as she walked out of my door.

"Who?"

"Read the profiles!" she shouted.

Elizabeth

Stepping onto the company jet was like stepping into another world. Each seat was oversized and looked more like a recliner you'd find in your home rather than a standard seat on an airplane. Mahogany workstations equipped with outlets and USB ports were positioned between two seats facing each other. I'd never flown on the jet alone before, and I felt almost ridiculous doing it, but I was thankful the higher ups allowed me to use it for this gathering. Having access to a private jet made traveling a hell of a lot easier.

A pretty brunette appeared at my side. "Can I get you something to drink, Miss Lyons?"

I pondered only for a moment before deciding that some alcohol wouldn't be the worst idea I'd ever had. Not wanting to smell like a brewery or arrive tipsy at the party, I made my decision. "I'd love a glass of wine."

"Of course. White or red?"

"White, please," I said, not wanting to speak at this event with red-stained teeth.

Once in the air, drink in hand, I attempted to open the envelope that Barbara had sent with me. Placing down my glass, I tore open the sealed folder with both hands. Twenty-nine profiles were inside, twenty of them men. Each profile contained a photograph with the person's name and age underneath as well as a brief biography and an analysis of what the company did for business and the person's role in it. Side note: Most of them owned the companies where they worked.

This is why I loved Barbara. I would never have had the time or the initiative to think about doing this, but she did. She always instinctively knew, sometimes even before I did, what I'd need to be prepared for an event like this. *She so deserved a raise.*

Reading through the twenty-nine profiles, I acquainted myself with the other top youngsters on the West Coast. Barbara had been right about Daniel Alexander. His picture showed that he was ridiculously hot, and I'd admit that his was the only profile I had studied more than once. He founded and ran a web-based company in San Francisco, and he had a penchant for starting up and investing in small firms before selling them for billions. That was billions with a B.

He graduated at the top of his class, and from the looks of it, he wouldn't do one thing for too long, which was a pretty common theme for the majority of tonight's attendees. Business-hopping was one thing I couldn't relate to when it came to my peers and their constant complaints about feeling unfulfilled.

I loved my job and the studio where I worked. It was never boring, and I was never bored. Aspects of my position sucked, and I disliked those immensely, but for the most part, every day would be different, and I loved being on the creative end of things. Creating art for people to consume inspired me.

As I walked onto the airstairs, wind ripped through my hair, blowing it in every direction. Each time I'd visited San Francisco in the past, I'd adored it, but honestly, I couldn't wait to get back home to Los Angeles. The gloom, gusty, and cold air enveloping the city was in direct conflict with all the vibrant energy lying within it. Basically, I loved the way the city and its inhabitants seemed so inexplicitly alive, but I hated freezing my ass off to experience it.

"You look very nice tonight, Miss Lyons." A driver dressed in a black-and-white suit offered me a hand as I reached the last step.

I glanced down at my black cocktail dress. It fit me snug and hugged my curves in all the right places without looking trashy. That was what happened when people made dresses based off your measurements. You would end up looking like a walking piece of art each time you stepped out of the house.

"Thank you. You look nice, too…" I paused as I waited for his name.

"Thomas," he said as he held open the car door for me and I scooted inside.

"You look nice, too, Thomas. Any idea where we're headed?"

He smiled as he fastened his seatbelt and started the engine. "Of course. We're going to Atherton. Have you ever been there?"

"No. Is it a hotel?"

"It's a city—well, a town actually. It's the richest one in the nation."

My eyes widened. Aside from San Francisco and Napa, I hadn't been to many actual cities in Northern California, so I wasn't familiar with the area. "In the nation? Seriously? How come I've never heard of it?"

"You wouldn't know it if you weren't from here. You'll love it though. It's beautiful. The houses are incredible. Even the older homes tend to have spectacular yards."

"It sounds like something out of a fairy tale." My mind recalled a script I'd read recently, describing an affluent town filled with lush green trees, large houses, and good-natured people.

"Wait until you see it."

His eyes crinkled in the rearview mirror, and I knew he was smiling.

My phone pinged, forcing me to look away from Thomas and at my phone. Glancing down, I noticed a text message alert from Barbara. Part of Barbara's job description required her to be on call twenty-four hours a day, seven days a week. That wasn't atypical for someone at my level, and I honestly tried to never use her that way unless it was an emergency. It was one thing that I chose to devote all my time toward work and climbing the studio ladder, but I believed it wasn't fair of me to put those expectations on my assistant.

Are you there yet? How's Daniel? Give him my phone number.

I chuckled to myself as I read her text and quickly typed out one of my own.

Not there yet. I'll not only give him your number, but I'll also write it on the bathroom wall. Wouldn't want to limit your options.

The businesswoman in me wanted to chastise herself for being so loose and carefree in a text message. I'd witnessed firsthand how anything in writing, in any form, could come back to haunt you.

When I'd worked in the writing department, one of the more senior writers had informed the entire room that he had been keeping every email from his superior and had printed and compiled them into a binder in case the messages ever got lost mysteriously on the company server. He'd eventually sued the studio for wrongful termination and he'd won a shitload of money. It was all because of, literally, a few measly sentences that had been written via email in the heat of a disagreement. *Had they been inappropriate? Sure. But hadn't we all done something as innocent as that to one another before?* I knew I had, and the thought terrified me.

It was that day when I'd realized that I would have to be careful about every single thing that I ever put into writing, in any form, to anyone. I'd censor my thoughts and my ideas, and I'd spend more time constructing HR-appropriate responses to each email. When words that could be misconstrued via email were required, I'd make sure they were only spoken in face-to-face conversations. It had been hard at first, and I had grown lax about it with the handful of people I trusted, people like Barbara.

Elizabeth

"Miss Lyons?"

Thomas's voice broke through my past thoughts.

"We're almost in town. I thought you might want to look around. It will be dark when we leave, and I wouldn't want you to miss it."

"Thank you," I said as my eyes fell upon oak-lined streets.

Most of the homes were set far enough back from the roadway that I couldn't see them, but I could tell when one was special. It was as though the trees knew it, too. They had grown tall and lush to protect all the magic that lived here, keeping it well hidden from prying eyes.

We pulled up to a gated drive, and Thomas checked a Post-it note stuck to the side of the passenger seat before punching in the required code. The wide gates swung open without a sound, and I audibly gasped at what appeared before us.

"Jesus, Thomas, this is stunning."

I looked around at the perfectly manicured garden with fountains and small sculptures adorning it. The front lawn alone was bigger than most of the lots in LA—unless you lived in Beverly Hills or Bel Air. Honestly, I sort of felt like I was in one of those cities as we pulled onto the stone-paved driveway.

The home itself was two stories, but it was wider instead of taller. The windows were lit up in every direction, nary a curtain or covering to be seen. The entire second story had a balcony edged in ornamental iron mixed with miniature cement columns. Gas lamps, all glowing and flickering in the softening daylight, hung evenly across the front of the first and second stories.

If one could fall in love with a house, I thought I did right then. "This is unbelievable," I commented to Thomas as he opened my door for me and offered his hand.

Upon exiting the car, I was met by another suit-clad gentleman carrying a silver tray of three champagne flutes. He offered me one before gesturing toward another well-dressed gentleman, who had suddenly appeared and moved to the car behind us.

"Good evening, Miss Lyons. I'm Shane," he said with a smile.

I noted that I hadn't told him my name yet. *Impressive*, I thought to myself.

"If you'll follow me," he jutted his elbow for me to hold before proceeding to walk me toward the entrance of the house.

I stared at the oversized double glass doors as we stopped in front of a giant of a man holding a clipboard. He looked like a bouncer who stood guard outside of dance clubs.

"David, this is Miss Lyons," Shane announced before removing my arm from his.

David scanned down his list and scribbled something with his pen before greeting me with a tight lipped smile.

"Miss Lyons, it's nice to see you. Please come in." He waved a hand inside. "Is there anything else you need?"

"The powder room?" I asked with my clutch tucked firmly against my side.

"Make a right after the Monet, and go through the double doors at the end of the hallway. It will be on your left."

"Thank you." I touched his arm in a polite gesture while trying to remember all the directions.

I swore, I looked down at the flooring for only a moment before I crashed into a hard body and spilled part of my drink.

"Shit, I'm sorry," I said before looking up and meeting light hazel eyes that instantly hypnotized me. *Why did they look so familiar?*

"I'm not." His voice was deep and throaty as his eyes raked me from head to toe with no shame.

Wiping the frown from my face, I regained my composure. "I was looking at the floor and not where I was walking. Did I get champagne on you?"

"I'm fine." He brushed a single droplet from his jacket sleeve. "I'm Daniel Alexander."

He extended his hand, and I forced myself to shake it.

"Of course you are," I said, slightly tossing back my head. *Barbara would love to hear this story tomorrow.*

"Oh, you know who I am? I'm impressed."

"Don't be. My assistant did all the research and then forced me to read it."

He laughed, and his face crinkled in a way that showed he did it a lot—laugh that was. Lines around his eyes creased like they were always there, and I found them charming. I stared at said lines as if they were magical beings, and I wondered what it was, or who, that made him laugh so often.

"See something you like?" he teased, breaking the spell I was under, as he cocked an eyebrow.

"Yeah, the floor," I said before glancing back down at it.

"Italian marble. Every inch of it was flown in from this tiny town in Italy. Beautiful, isn't it?"

How the hell did he know that? "It is. I was thinking about how it looks exactly as I pictured from a script I recently read. It's almost like the story was talking about this particular house."

"Maybe it was," he offered simply.

"Or maybe I've just found my perfect location for the interior and exterior home shots," I bit back with more fire in my tone than I had intended.

His mouth upturned into a cocky half smile. "You talk to your boyfriend with that mouth?"

I shook my head at his ridiculous question. "Is that your way of asking me if I'm single?"

"Are you?"

"Why do you care?"

"'Cause I want to know." He blinked once before refocusing his hazel gaze on me. "Do you have a boyfriend?"

"No, and I'm not looking for one either—you know, if that was your next question."

Daniel laughed again. "Feisty. Most women aren't feisty around me."

"Let me guess, they drop their panties at the mere sight of you?" The thought had crossed my mind.

He leaned in close to me, his mouth nearing my ear. "Usually."

"How charming and wonderful for you to get off so easily—pun intended." Normally, I wouldn't behave so crass at a professional event, but Daniel's ego seemed to bring out the best in me. Instead of berating myself for being so cavalier around him, I made a mental note that I never planned on seeing or speaking to him again, so my attitude couldn't hurt. I turned away to find the powder room, suddenly remembering where I was headed before running into Mr. Super Hot Distraction.

My forward movement stopped with a jerk as he tugged on my arm. "I never ask them to act like that. They just do. And I never said I take them up on it either."

"Oh, I'm sure you sit at home every night with your dick in your hands, wondering what on earth to do with it." I rolled my eyes, not believing a word he'd said.

"I never said that either. I fuck, Elizabeth, and I do it often. But it's with women I trust and have known for years."

"Wait, what? How do you know my name?" I stumbled through my question.

"You're not the only one who did the homework."

Cute. Damn it, he's cute.

"As I was saying, I only sleep with women I've known for a long time."

"I don't remember asking," I halted his declaration in a desperate attempt to make him stop talking so that I could force my gaze away from his mouth.

He laughed. "You wanted to know."

I did.

"I really didn't," I played.

"Well, just for future reference, I never sleep with any random panty-droppers I meet out."

"Like I said before, how charming. Now, if you'll excuse me." I pulled my arm out of his grasp and walked straight ahead, pretending that I wasn't flustered and completely turned on by his touch.

"Don't I get credit for having friends with benefits?" he shouted at my retreating back.

I stopped mid-stride. "You're joking, right?"

"No. I mean, isn't that better than screwing whatever walks?"

"It's funny because I bet you think these women don't have feelings for you. Do you have any idea how we function?" I found myself growing more and more flustered with each word he'd spoken.

He stepped toward me as his eyes roamed down the length of my body. I stopped myself from shivering, and I crossed my arms in front of my chest instead.

"I have a pretty good idea about how you function."

"Then, you're an even bigger idiot than you look. Bet you a hundred bucks that at least one of them is in love with you." I smacked my lips closed and jutted my hip.

His head drew back slightly as he frowned. "No way. Feelings are not in the arrangement."

"You seriously think not one of your"—I cleared my throat and lowered my voice—"fuck buddies isn't hoping you'll change your mind about her eventually?"

"No way," he responded with confidence.

"Girls always want to be the chosen one, especially with the type of guy who never settles down. We love being the one who you change all your rules for. We live for that shit. And if we think there's even a remote chance in hell of that happening, we'll stick around and wait for you to realize it. It's in our DNA."

"Now, who's the idiot?" he said with a laugh, clearly not believing a thing I said.

"Still you 'cause you know I'm right. If you don't, then you're even dumber than I originally thought." I turned on my heel and hustled to the bathroom before closing the door behind me.

Daniel

Elizabeth disappeared behind the restroom door. She was feisty with a foul little mouth, and she was a fucking eyeful. She'd stunned me in that little black dress that looked like it had been made for her. Her tits swelled out the top, and the way her hips curved had made my dick wake up and take notice.

I waited in the hallway, frustrated that she hadn't let me respond to her ludicrous assumptions. Granted, she was probably right about the majority of women, considering she was one. *But what did she know about the two women I was fucking? Nothing.*

The women in my life knew exactly what we had between us—a no-strings, no-drama, purely sex-based arrangement. It couldn't be classified as a relationship, and I never romanced them for the exact reasons Elizabeth had mentioned. You shouldn't get me wrong. I wasn't a dick to them or anything. I just didn't do things like buy gifts or send flowers or shit like that.

Neither of the girls ever attended events with me. I always went to functions alone, solo, single, party of uno because I never wanted to give them the wrong idea or lead them on. I had been upfront from day one, and absolutely nothing had changed in the years since we'd been hooking up off and on—safely, I might add.

I always used protection.

Girls can be crazy.

So, Elizabeth's assumptions pissed me off and riled me up—if I believed them, that was, which I didn't. I convinced myself that her rant had nothing to do with me and everything to do with her. She was wrong, so wrong, and most likely, she had projected a failed relationship onto me.

I bet she'd wanted to change a guy once before, and it hadn't worked out in her favor. He had probably been upfront from the beginning, but she never wanted to hear it, or she'd refused to believe him. When it had finally ended—his decision, of course—her heart had shattered, and he'd walked away pain free.

Idiot.

From my research, I had noticed that she wasn't married. Yes, I'd checked. When I'd double-checked her left hand to see if an engagement ring sat on the proper finger, I'd breathed out a fucking sigh of relief when I found it empty. Relief! I recognized this gut feeling in me instantly even though it had been years since I genuinely felt it.

I wanted her.

I fucking wanted her.

From the second she'd spilled her drink on me, I'd wanted to rip that tightly fitted dress right off her body and show her how well I'd fit her instead.

I should have walked away. The second she shut the restroom door, I should have bolted.

But I hadn't.

I couldn't.

Elizabeth

After blotting my face and fixing my makeup, I opened the restroom door to see Daniel standing there, leaning against the wall with his hand running across the scruff on his cheeks. "What are you doing?"

"Waiting for you."

"Why?" I asked, my tone annoyed. I headed back toward the grand ballroom—or at least the direction I assumed was the right way.

"For such a smart girl, you sure ask a lot of stupid questions."

I stopped walking and turned to face him. My finger poking against his taut chest, I said, "I never claimed to be smart, and you're the stupid one. Go find some other girl who will give you her panties."

"I told you, I don't fuck strangers."

"Then, what the hell do you want?"

"He must have really screwed you over." Daniel's breath was hot against my cheek, and I swatted him away, determined not to give in.

"He who?"

"The one who made you hate men."

"I don't hate men."

"Then, why are you so angry?"

"Maybe you're just annoying."

"Maybe you just hate men," he fired back, the words drawn-out and deliberate.

"I told you, I don't hate men."

"Just me then? It's just me you can't stand?" He smirked, and his laugh lines reappeared.

Who the hell is this guy?

"I don't even know you, and you sure as shit don't know me, so stop making assumptions," I growled before practically sprinting away from him.

Was I truly that transparent?

I hadn't thought about Ben for years, but the minute Daniel had mentioned the one who *screwed me over*, I'd seen it all fresh in my mind again as if it happened an hour ago—pink panties stuck on her foot, chipped nail polish on the table, his face covered in her, his mouth spewing those soul-slashing words. I shuddered at the memory.

That moment had defined me. It was in that moment, standing in the entryway of my apartment, that I'd decided I would never be the kind of girl who gave up her hopes and dreams for a guy. I'd realized that no guy would ever be worth that kind of self-sacrifice, and no guy of worth would ever ask that of me.

If even half of what Ben had spewed that day was accurate, I'd decided that I would rather be alone forever than be with someone who wanted me to change who I was. Accepting that the majority of men wouldn't be able to handle me and my passion for my job, I'd convinced myself that I was perfectly okay with that.

And I had been.

I was.

Elizabeth

I spent the rest of the evening avoiding Daniel Alexander—or at least I tried to. I forced myself into awkward conversations with the other attendees, none of whom held even half the charm in their entire bodies that Daniel was blessed with in his pinky.

How had I gotten roped into this event again? Each person was supposed to be fascinating, smart, interesting, ambitious, driven, and young Mostly, they were superficially arrogant, socially awkward, or inherently competitive. These were all traits I found completely undesirable, especially in settings like this one where I couldn't sneak away and find refuge in a restroom away from the chaos until the night ended—without my absence being noticed, that was.

"Dance with me," Daniel suddenly cooed in my ear.

I scowled. "No."

"Just one dance," he all but begged, pulling me away from a small group of event sponsors.

I glanced out at the merely empty dance floor. "No." I paused. "But thank you."

I wasn't sure why Daniel seemed so hell-bent on bothering me, but I was flustered. I hadn't felt this way—hell, I hadn't felt *any way* for a guy in a really long time. I was pretty sure that Daniel Alexander was the last person on earth I wanted to go and have feelings for, attraction or otherwise. He had *heartbreaker* written all over his stupidly gorgeous body.

Grabbing my hand, he eased me onto the dance floor. He moved one hand tight against my lower back while the other clutched mine in perfect dance form.

"Did you not get told *no* often enough as a kid or something?"

I tried to pull away from him, but he only gripped me tighter as the orchestral music filtered throughout the room.

"I heard no plenty. I just don't want to hear it from you."

"Oh my God, are you a caveman?" Part of me flushed with want, and the other part fought back with repulsion. "Do you carry a club? Are you going to hit me over the head with it?" I looked around at his sides, my eyes searching for the mock weapon.

"Very funny." He smirked and twirled me effortlessly across the dance floor, his moves fluid and his body strong.

I felt safe in his arms, and an unfamiliar feeling of longing soared through me.

"I just know what I want, Elizabeth, and I have a hard time letting go."

"What are you saying exactly?" I cocked my head to the side and looked into his hazel eyes.

"You need me to spell it out for you?"

He winked and dipped me low, causing my head to fall back. I squealed in response to the sudden shifting of my weight before a giggle slipped out. Daniel's lips brushed over my ear, and my eyes closed automatically in response.

"I want you."

My eyes shot open as I placed both feet on the ground and righted my body. "You can't possibly mean that. You know nothing about me."

"You're exactly the type of woman I want to get to know better."

My body chilled as excitement spiked through me. The idea of doing anything with this man was tempting, but I had to remain focused. Glancing over to the side of the room, my eyes were met with glares from the other few women in attendance.

"Looks like you have a fan club." I nudged my head in the direction of my now glowering female attendees.

"I'm well aware."

"Are you always this cocky?"

"Are you always this difficult? I just wanted to dance with you, and you told me no."

His thumb moved up and down on my hand, and I lost all focus.

"Now, I tell you that I want to get to know you better, and you deny me. You keep running away from me, Elizabeth, and I don't like it."

"So?"

"So…" He paused before leaning in and breathing in the scent of my neck. "Stop running."

"Stop chasing." I smiled.

He loosened his grip, and catching him off guard, I left him alone on the dance floor.

Elizabeth

After shoving away from Daniel's body, I quickly moved toward a small group of esteemed male guests. Their conversation came to an abrupt halt as soon as I appeared. Sensing the uncomfortable air that had obviously followed my presence, I smiled politely and excused myself.

Now was the perfect time to seek out that restroom refuge I so desperately needed. Once inside, I sat on the ledge of the ornate pedestal tub. I focused on my breathing, berating myself for being so attracted to Daniel and enjoying his Neanderthal advances.

Hadn't I learned my lesson back in college? Over the years, I had convinced myself that Ben was right about men and the kind of women they wanted by their sides, and I wasn't it.

A loud knock startled me, and I almost fell into the tub I was perched on the edge of.

"Almost done," I announced with a stutter, cursing under my breath that my safe haven had been discovered.

"Just let me in, Elizabeth." Daniel's voice breathed out through the doorframe.

After hesitating for a moment, I pushed off the ledge and clicked the door's lock. He opened the door and stepped in before locking it again behind him. All the while, he eyed me, his head shaking.

"Why are you hiding in here?" he asked.

I returned to my tub of solitude. "Why are you always following me?"

"Maybe I find you interesting." He took a step toward me, closing the small space between us.

"Maybe I find you irritating."

"You don't." He knelt in front of me.

His head was still slightly above mine, causing me to look up in order to eye him.

"I most certainly do."

"I don't believe you," he said before placing a hand on my waist and pulling my weight forward, causing me to grip the tub for balance.

His lips crushed against mine before I could protest. And holy shit, I did not want to protest, no matter how many warning bells rang in my ears. My mouth opened, allowing his tongue to enter. His free hand ran up the length of my dress and stopped on my chest before taking a handful of my breast and squeezing. He moaned into my mouth, and I reached out to remove his jacket with my hands before groping his chest and abs.

Jesus. Was it legal to be that smart, successful, and toned?

"How do you have time to work out?" I blurted into his mouth.

He pulled away, wearing a cocky smirk. "Come again?"

"I haven't yet. But I was asking, how do you have time to work out? I don't have time to eat dinner, much less anything else."

I'd spend nearly all my time at the office or doing something for the studio, like attending functions, events, press releases, junctions, and so on. When I did attend a business meal, I would spend the majority of it speaking about our latest project or answering a million questions about the speed of production and the potential cost of delays. Usually, I'd only have one or two bites by the time the meal ended.

"Well, sometimes, I get a chance to run, but that's about it," I added.

"I make time, and so should you."

I leaned back, my body arching away from his touch. "Did you just call me fat?"

He laughed. The deep and throaty sound bewitched me all the way into my girlie parts.

"Do I look fucking stupid?"

Shrugging, I cocked my head to one side and warningly eyed him.

"I wasn't talking about the working-out part. By all accounts, you don't need it."

He licked his lips, and I stopped myself from panting.

"I only meant that you should make time for things like dinner. Food's important, being fuel and all that."

"Overrated."

"Better in bed."

"You are such a guy."

"Thanks for noticing."

Standing up, I adjusted my dress and made one last mirror check before turning toward Daniel. "I really should get going. I have a flight to catch."

"Stay." His hand caressed the back of mine as he rose to his feet.

My heart raced inside my chest at his offer that sounded too good to be true. Even if he did mean it, I couldn't. Men like him were a distraction. Listening to my heart was stupid, and I refused to ever be stupid again, no matter how much my heart pounded in defiance against my chest.

This industry was waiting for me to fall apart, to do something dumb, to lose it all, and I had to reject anything that could possibly help that happen. Daniel Alexander could make me lose sight of everything I'd worked so hard for. While in his presence, I seemed to lose all ability to say no to him.

"I thought you didn't do this kind of thing?" I asked.

"I'll make an exception." He smiled, seeming sincere.

I almost believed him. "I won't," I said as I unlatched the lock on the door.

"This isn't over. I'm not letting you walk away from me that easily."

"Sure looks like it to me." I walked out, leaving Daniel to watch me go.

Daniel

Goddamn. Watching Elizabeth Lyons's ass walk away from me was one of the hottest things I'd witnessed all year, and I'd seen a lot of hot shit.

I knew what she was trying to do by avoiding me. She assumed I was bad news. It was the normal first impression of me, no matter what I would do or say. When it came to women, I was often told that I *reeked of trouble*—whatever the hell that meant. Although, to be honest, it usually only fueled their desire for me. *What could I say?* It seemed that women not only liked trouble, they fucking loved it. And they loved fucking it.

But not her.

Elizabeth was focused. She had probably dealt with more come-ons in her industry than I cared to imagine. This wasn't a game to her.

After spending more time with her tonight, I sensed that her actions were pure, her reactions to me sincere. She wasn't the type of girl who fucked around. Actually, she didn't seem like the type of girl who fucked at all. She had come off as sort of repressed, but she'd tried to hide all that behind a sassy mouth. *God, what a mouth it was.*

Kissing her had challenged my willpower. Hell, being in the same room with her had challenged my fucking willpower. I wanted to unrepress her, undress her, and whatever else she'd let me do. I knew that wouldn't be much of anything, so I'd restrained myself the best I could. A man could only be so strong when faced with temptation and desire.

That kiss had to happen. I refused to let her leave tonight without giving her something to miss. I was attracted to her on a primal level. Her body was like an instrument made purely for my hands, and I found myself unable to stay away, no matter how hard I tried.

But there was more to her than that, depth and substance to a degree that I wasn't accustomed to in my lifestyle, even though I constantly looked for it. Female attention was always easy for me to come by, so that wasn't the problem. Not to mention, having the reputation I did in the Bay Area had landed me on more than one of the hottest Bay Area bachelor lists.

As much as I hated those fucking things because of the unwanted attention they'd bring me, they would also introduce me to some new business ventures I wouldn't have had otherwise, so I couldn't write them off completely. But I could do without the trashy, classless, and money-hungry women who always appeared right after those articles.

You shouldn't get me wrong. I was not a fucking angel by any means, but I was trying. I used to love dipping my dick into any pussy that would let me. It was certainly crude, but it had once been the truth.

In the earlier days of my success, I had absolutely been the kind of guy who tripped face-first into any and every hot piece of ass that passed by. She couldn't hold a conversation about anything other than clothes and makeup? I couldn't care less. All she had going for her were her model good looks and legs that refused to quit? Perfect. Wrap those babies around my shoulders. She never graduated from college or had any vital life experience? Hot, sweaty sex didn't need a degree the last time I'd checked.

I had been, by all means, a typical red-blooded American male. A wealthy, ambitious, attractive, and young guy, I'd worked my ass off by day and screwed my dick off by night—not literally, thank God.

My record-setting pace hadn't taken long to catch up with me, and I'd eventually had the scare of my up-to-that-point life.

A one-night stand had waltzed into my place of employment—luckily, I owned it—and demanded to see me. She had all but thrown a hissy fit in the lobby of my busy building. The moment she had seen me, she'd broken down into tears, sobbing, while I'd scoured the recesses of my mind, trying to remember her name or where exactly I'd met her.

She'd started screaming about sleeping with me and being late, and before my brain could catch up with whatever the hell she had been trying to tell me, she'd blurted out that she was pregnant. My world had spun, and I'd lost all focus as I grasped on to the receptionist's desk to keep my knees from buckling.

Ladies, if you ever wanted to scare the ever-loving shit out of a man you'd just met, you should tell him you were pregnant with his kid. I didn't say that to be cruel. It was just honest. The scariest moment I'd had in my life was when I'd thought that I had gotten someone I didn't know at all pregnant.

Sparing the gory details, the girl—whose name was Lori by the way—had admitted she lied about the pregnancy. She had concocted the scheme to either extort an exuberant amount of money from me or to get me to marry her, either resulting in the same ending, money after the inevitable divorce. Neither had worked, considering the size of the legal team I had at my disposal. They had quickly determined that she was a filthy liar, so I'd filed a restraining order.

The day of the scare, I'd stopped sleeping around with strangers. That little nightmare down Almost Daddy Lane had been enough to pretty much kill my libido, and I could swear that my dick had experienced a mental breakdown in the lobby of that old building because he hadn't been quite the same ever since. He still worked and got his rocks off, but it wasn't without a lot of help on my end.

That was, until tonight.

Tonight, he'd woken up all on his own, and I'd never been so happy to see him. I had been half-tempted to throw him a welcome-home party, but I digressed.

Elizabeth Lyons had woken up the sleeping dragon, and now, she'd have to deal with it.

Elizabeth

I made sure to get into the office extra early. The fact that I had barely slept after I'd gotten home last night might have something to do with it. Daniel had riled me up, and knowing he was about five hundred miles away from me had done nothing to settle my nerves.

"You didn't fall in love and stay the night? I'm so disappointed." Barbara's voice filtered into my office, and the sound of desk drawers opening and closing quickly followed.

"I'm here, aren't I?" I stepped out of my door and into the quiet hallway.

I enjoyed being at the studio before the rest of the crew got in, and everyone's ears perked at the slightest bit of personal talk or gossip.

"How was he? You're…"

She eyeballed me, and I suddenly wanted to go hide in my closet.

"Oh my God, you're flushed. Did you bring him back with you or something? Is he in your office?"

I laughed out loud. "What on God's green earth are you talking about?"

"Daniel Alexander. He was by far the only guy worth drooling over at that mixer. So, tell me everything." Her voice rose in pitch with her excitement level. "And I swear to God, Elizabeth, if you leave out a single detail, I'll know. My vagina will tell me."

"Shut the hell up. What is wrong with you?" I whisper-shouted at her through my tight-lipped smile as I leaned in.

She swatted my shoulder. "It's fine. HR isn't even in yet. No one's here. Now, tell me everything."

"I wasn't even talking about HR." I rolled my eyes at my insane assistant, whom I loved dearly.

Even though she was a crazed lunatic, she was *my* crazed lunatic. We walked into the kitchen, and she grabbed coffee while I piled fruit onto a plate.

"You were right about Daniel. He was hot, so hot," I informed her.

"Anyone with eyeballs could see that. What was he like?"

I tried to think of how to classify Daniel. *What words would describe him best?* "I don't know. He was bossy and arrogant and irritating. He pretty much stalked me all night."

Sipping her coffee, she almost choked as she quickly swallowed. "Oh my God, you like him."

"Nope."

"You do."

"I don't."

"Do."

"Ugh," I groaned. "You sound just like him. Maybe you two should date. It would be like elementary school all over again."

"I'm hurt." She placed a hand over her heart. "I would never move in on a man you liked. You know I'm not that kind of lady."

"I don't even know him. Even though I think he's hot, it doesn't matter. You know my rule, Barbara—no guys."

I wanted to forget about last night. Daniel Alexander could continue living his über successful life up in San Francisco, and I could pretend that he didn't exist. This was the best option for me anyway, considering I couldn't get him out of my damn head since I'd walked away from him.

My rules—or one rule actually—consisted of no dating and no distractions until I made a solid name for myself at this company and in this industry. I realized that I'd already made a splash that most people would kill for, but that was because of my age and title, not necessarily because of my work.

Everyone was waiting for me to fail, for the journalistic articles on my talent to be baseless and untrue. Most of the people whom I considered friends at one time had talked shit behind my back. When people spoke about the entertainment industry being filled with those who would step all over others to get ahead, they had no idea how much truth lied in that statement. And the men were worse than the women in that regard. The men would gossip and plot in ways that honestly scared me. I had to keep my wits about me at all times, or I'd be done for.

The worst part was, these men who wanted me out of this position didn't even know why—other than the fact that I was a female. My work truly did speak for itself, and they all knew it. They simply couldn't handle it.

All I really craved was respect from an industry that had always been a boys' club. I wanted everyone to know what they were getting when they worked with me—a talented, on-top-of-things, undistracted, kick-ass executive who could do the job better than anyone had before. So, until that day arrived, there would be no distractions.

Truthfully, up until last night, that rule had been easy to adhere to. I rarely met anyone who wasn't business-related, and I never mixed business with pleasure.

When I'd happened to meet men, most were intimidated by my success and couldn't get away from me quickly enough. It usually took all of two minutes into a conversation before a guy would check his phone for messages, looking for a way out.

As disappointing as those times had been, I never let them get to me because I hadn't been interested in any of those men in the first place. I'd only spoken to them initially to prove that asshole Ben wrong. I wanted to be desired for my ambition and talent, not feared for it. But all I'd ended up doing was proving him right time and time again, and that had only solidified my realization that guys, for the most part, sucked.

That was, until Daniel Alexander had waltzed into my life and made me feel. He'd kissed my lips, and I'd not only let him, but I'd also enjoyed it. Hell, I couldn't stop daydreaming about it. It was as though this guy had reached into my chest, grabbed my heart with one hand, and squeezed until it started beating again. My heart, which had lain dormant for so long, was now wide-awake.

"Hello?"

The sound of fingers snapping drew me out of my thoughts.

"Earth to Elizabeth." Barbara waved a hand in front of my face.

"I'm sorry. I spaced for a second. What were you saying?" I tried to play it cool, like nothing had just happened and that I hadn't gone into a Daniel-space zone.

Hearts were too sensitive, too easily swayed if not properly protected. That organ could fuck everything up for me if I allowed it. I had to stop thinking about Daniel and his stupid, perfect lips.

"I was saying," she paused for a moment, "that your rules are dumb. One day, you're going to meet someone who will show you exactly that and you'll break those damn rules without a second thought. Then, what?"

I sighed a long, drawn-out overdramatic sound. "I guess we'll see *if* that ever happens, but it won't 'cause I won't let it."

"You can't control everything in your life."

"Wanna bet?"

"You'll see. You're going to want a partner, your other half. You'll want love." Her tone turned serious as her face looked almost forlorn.

I nodded to make her feel better. "You're probably right. But I don't want it right now. I truly don't care about any of that. I'm so fulfilled in other ways that truly matter to me that I don't miss what everyone else thinks I should be looking for."

"Okay, I get that, but, you seem to hate the very idea of it."

"Of what? A relationship?"

"Love. You hate love," she said the words so effortlessly.

I wanted to cringe from just hearing them. They reminded me of what Daniel had said about me hating men.

"I do not," I tried to argue, but it was no use.

"Don't lie to me."

"If I were a guy, we wouldn't even be having this conversation. You'd be encouraging me to go out and screw everything that walked, and then you'd high-five me every time I did."

Her eyebrows pulled together as her face scrunched. "Uh…I'm still encouraging you to go out and screw everything that walks, and I'd do more than high-five you. I'd buy you a damn cookie."

"I do like cookies." I glanced up at the ceiling tiles, pondering her idea.

"See? That's motivation to meet men and break your rules—cookies!"

"Seriously, Barbara, the last thing I need in my life right now is a stupid, needy man. I'm busy enough without having to think about someone else's schedule."

Of course, I'd already thought about someone else's schedule all last night and all this morning. Daniel had infected my mind with his eyes and lips.

"What are you babbling on about?"

"Just all the stuff that goes along with being in a relationship. You know what I mean. I don't miss checking in with someone all the time or asking for permission or running things by another person or taking his feelings into consideration on every stupid little detail. It's so much work, and I have enough work."

"When did you get so unromantic?" she whined, dramatically throwing her head back.

I could pinpoint two exact occasions, and Barbara already knew about one, but I kept the other locked inside.

Shrugging at her would have to suffice for an answer.

"I know Ben really hurt you—" she started to say.

I put a hand up to stop her. "That stuff with Ben happened forever ago."

"Doesn't mean it didn't scar you."

"I don't want to talk about this anymore." I pouted.

10
Elizabeth

Aside from dipshit Ben, my faith in love had been all but shattered when I watched my parents' marriage crumble before my eyes. My mom had supported my dad all through law school. Then, she had been there for him as he built his company from nothing, and it had grown to be one of the biggest and most respected law firms in the LA area. I always felt like if there had been a poster for "Behind every great man is an even greater woman," my mom would have modeled for it.

What my mother and myself hadn't counted on was my dad leaving his perfectly supportive wife for one of his law firm interns. When he'd first announced it to the two of us over a rare family dinner, which I'd driven home from college for, I'd thought it was a joke. My head couldn't possibly comprehend what the hell he had just said.

"Janet"—*he glanced at my mom*— *"Elizabeth"*—*and then at me before returning his line of fire to my mother*— *"I'm leaving."*

"Oh, do you need to get back to the office?" My mom stood, most likely to pack up a to-go container of food for him to take back with him.

"No. I mean, I'm leaving this family, as in moving out. I've fallen in love with someone else. You've been a great wife, Janet, but it's time to move on."

Nothing.

There were no sounds, not even the air being sucked into anyone's lungs before being released.

I sure as shit wasn't breathing at this point.

More silence.

There was only the ticking of the clock on the wall.

Bitter silence was all around us as started to sink in.

I fought the churning in my stomach. I wished I could envelop my poor mother inside a rainbow-filled bubble where all the words my dad had so carelessly spewed at her would get sucked right out and explode into nothing. The funny thing about words was that you couldn't unhear them once they'd been spoken.

My mom bolted from the kitchen table, her legs shaking, as she ran crookedly toward the bathroom. The door slammed, and I was certain she was losing the contents of everything she'd just spent hours making.

"This is a joke, right? Is it April first?" I tilted my head toward the wall, searching desperately for the calendar my mom always kept there. I silently prayed it was a month in which I knew it wasn't.

"Grow up, Elizabeth. Things like this happen every day. People fall in and out of love. Nothing lasts forever. You're an adult, for Christ's sake. This shouldn't even affect you."

"An adult? Jesus, Dad, I'm nineteen!"

"Old enough to get over it."

"Or old enough to be scarred forever."

"Always so dramatic. You sure you don't want to be an actress? Love is fleeting, Elizabeth. It's better you learn that now before you think you've found it."

His eyes steeled, and I felt something inside me break beyond repair.

I steadied my nerves and tried to temper my anger. "How could you tell Mom like that? It was really inconsiderate and cruel."

My dad sucked in a breath, and then he wiped his mustache with a cloth napkin before placing it on top of his plate. "No sense in beating around the bush or dragging it out. I did your mother a favor by telling her this way."

"Your idea of favors is fucked." I placed a hand on my stomach, praying that my own dinner contents would stay right where they were.

"Watch your mouth, young lady. I'll give you a twenty-four-hour pass to act like a spoiled brat, but then I expect you to get over this and move on. I want you to have dinner with Chris and me later this week."

"Who the fuck is Chris? Are you leaving Mom for a dude? 'Cause that might go over better." I noticed the odd sliver of relief making its way inside me.

"Absolutely not. A dude?" he breathed out, taking a sip of his wine. "You kids these days. Chris is short for Christina."

"Of course it is."

Note to self: Never shorten your name.

I had never planned on shortening my name, considering I most certainly didn't look like a Liz or Lizzie, but that just reaffirmed my position on the matter.

"And you're fucking insane if you think I'm going to dinner with you and the homewrecker."

"I've had enough disrespect for one night!" He slammed his wine goblet on the table, and the contents splashed out, staining the tablecloth. "Call me when you pull your head out of your ass."

"I dare you to hold your breath!" I shouted at his cowardice.

As I watched his retreating back, I wished the whole time that he would do what I dared and then keel over from the wait.

Asshole.

A too-smiley-for-this-early-in-the-morning assistant, whose name I couldn't quite remember, popped into the kitchen. "Good morning, Barbara and Miss Lyons." She was downright giddy.

"Good morning, Jeannie," Barbara added her name for my benefit.

"Morning," I said with a smile.

Jeannie reached for a coffee cup, and Barbara inhaled a sharp breath.

"Jeannie! What is on your finger?"

Jeannie half-screamed in the tiny kitchen before shooting me an apologetic look. She thrust her left hand in Barbara's face. "I got engaged last night! Isn't it gorgeous?"

Barbara's face lit up. "It is. Oh, it's so pretty. Isn't it, Elizabeth?"

The little wench pulled Jeannie's ring under my nose and forced me to look at it. It was stunning. There was no doubt about that.

"It's really sparkly. Congratulations," I offered.

"Yes! Congratulations. I want to hear all about what happened and your plans later, okay?" Barbara gave her a quick hug before exiting the room with me.

Once back in the safety cocoon of my office, Barbara started laughing. "Oh my God, you should have seen your face! It was priceless."

"What?" I asked, genuinely confused.

"I don't even know what the right word is." She started snapping her fingers as if the action would help the word come to her. "Indifferent! That's it. You're so indifferent to all this stuff that normal girls go gaga over."

I guessed the snapping had worked.

"I'm not indifferent. I'm happy for that girl I don't even know who looks all of twenty-two."

"She's twenty-three."

"Oh my God, why?" I fell back onto my couch, my head resting against the cushions.

"Why what?" Barbara's face still held the giant smile that had been plastered on her face since seeing *the* ring.

She fell onto the couch next to me as I inhaled and tried to word my thoughts correctly. I said, "You don't think that's a little young to get married? I look back at when I was twenty-three, and it wasn't even that long ago, but I've changed so much since then."

Barbara lifted a shoulder and made a soft noise. "I don't know. I would never have done it, but I think some people were just made to get married young—not us though." She nudged her shoulder into mine for solidarity.

"Not us is right."

"And you're okay with that?" Her big doe eyes searched mine for understanding.

"With what? Not going out every night, searching for a husband?"

She laughed again. "Not in those words necessarily, but yeah."

"Of course I'm okay with that. I just don't get why it seems like that's every girl's main goal in life. I mean, I get why they want to find love, but what I don't get is the priority of it. You know, that urgency—if it doesn't happen by a certain time or date, their lives are essentially over." I looked at her for confirmation that what I was saying wasn't completely asinine.

"You know it's your fault," she said matter-of-factly.

I guffawed. "My fault?"

"The entertainment industry—the movies we see, the books and magazines we read and the music we listen to. It all perpetuates this subliminal message to girls and boys and their roles in life. You know that."

I sighed. "I know, and I don't even want to get into that subject today. My brain already hurts. Plus, I'm pretty sure my girlie DNA is busted somewhere along my genetic path, and that's why I don't have this overwhelming desire for love in my life right now."

"You're definitely busted all right."

"I don't even care." I smiled. "Busted and successful. Busted and wealthy. Busted and happy. Alone. Without a man. Imagine that," I teased as I pushed up from the couch and walked toward my desk. *Why was it so hard to believe that someone could be happy alone?*

The sound of my office phone ringing caused Barbara to jump up and run out to her desk. "Elizabeth Lyons's office. This is Barbara."

I waited to hear what she would say next, as I looked at my calendar for the meetings of the day. I had one hour until the first one, and I still needed to prep the latest box-office numbers, double-check the movies in preproduction, and meet with my managers to make sure our own production schedule was on track.

Barbara's giggling voice filtered into my office.

Who the hell was making my assistant laugh like that? I had an idea, but why would he be calling me?

"Stop it, Mr. Alexander. Let me see if she's in. Would you mind holding?"

I heard another giggle as she peered through my open doorway.

"Daniel Alexander's on the phone for you." She was practically foaming at the mouth.

"I'm busy," I said, pretending not to be the least bit interested even though my entire body flushed with excitement.

"Seriously? You don't want to talk to him?"

Yes. "Nope."

"I don't think playing hard to get is going to work on him." She rolled her eyes before disappearing.

"I'm not playing," I said out loud to my empty office.

But I was, and I damn well knew it.

Elizabeth

I sorted through the paperwork currently shooting out of my printer when a new email pinged. Spinning my chair around to face my desk, I noticed the sender's name right away, and chills raced through my body.

FROM: ALEXANDER, DANIEL

TO: LYONS, ELIZABETH

SUBJECT: STILL THINKING...

MISS LYONS,

I CAN'T STOP THINKING ABOUT THAT KISS LAST NIGHT. TELL ME WE'LL GET TO DO IT AGAIN—SOON.

—DANIEL

Was he for real? I immediately hit the Reply button and stared at my computer screen for what felt like hours, but I knew that only seconds had passed. Part of me wanted to respond with something snarky and emasculating just for fun, but the rest of me knew that any response would only encourage him further. *How could I respond to something that mentioned a kiss over company email anyway?*

I had to ignore him—or try.

But I had tried to ignore him last night, and we'd seen how well that worked out—strong arms swinging me around the dance floor, his lips on mine.

Ugh!

I should have forced Barbara to call him and bitch him out for being so unprofessional, but he'd probably like that. I had a feeling that Daniel Alexander liked anything anyone told him not to do. Shaking my head, I closed the email without responding, but I didn't delete it. I didn't have time for this guy, but Lord, how I wanted to make some.

No! I silently berated myself for being so conflicted when it came to him. He was quickly becoming a weakness I couldn't afford.

My email pinged again.

FROM: ALEXANDER, DANIEL

TO: LYONS, ELIZABETH

SUBJECT: SILENCE

YOUR SILENCE IS KILLING ME. DON'T MAKE ME DO SOMETHING RASH TO GET YOUR ATTENTION.

—DANIEL

Really? My silence had occurred in the last twenty seconds since I received his first email. This man needed a lesson in patience, not to mention accepting the word *no*. I would add it to the mental list I'd so clearly started keeping on what Daniel needed lessons in. *Damn it!*

Barbara eyed me as I hustled between meetings. Carrying a stack of production papers and two new scripts, I rushed into my office to deposit them before grabbing the folder I needed for my next meeting.

I stopped short the second I entered. A sea of red swarmed atop my desk, and I spied what were easily at least two-dozen long-stemmed roses. My eyes focused in on the single white rose standing in the center of the bunch. This was the most beautiful flower arrangement I'd ever received.

I walked calmly toward them even though my insides urged me to sprint there. Leaning down to inhale the fragrance, I touched the petals of the white rose, admiring it the most.

Reaching for the tiny envelope, I opened it and pulled out the card.

IN A ROOMFUL OF ROSES,

YOU'RE THE ONLY ONE I SEE.

PLEASE LET ME SEE YOU AGAIN.

—DANIEL

"You're in trouble now," Barbara's voice warned, pulling me out of my rose-filled trance.

I glanced up at her, knowing full well how right she was but refusing to admit it.

Daniel

Between calls and meetings, I stared at my computer for most of the day, waiting for Elizabeth's name to show up in my inbox or on my telephone caller ID. But that never happened. Every hour that had passed with no response from her drove me more and more crazy. I was used to being in control, but she made me feel helpless.

I fought off the urge to text her, knowing that she'd most likely ignore that as well, and I couldn't handle any more rejection from her today. She'd also wonder how I'd gotten her number, and I refused to rat out her assistant, who was quickly becoming my biggest ally.

Checking the tracking number one last time, I knew the roses had been received at 3:17 p.m., and someone in the main security office had signed for them. *Maybe Elizabeth hadn't seen them yet?* I was half-tempted to call Barbara to check, but I stopped myself from wanting to know the truth. *What would it mean if she'd seen them but not reached out to me?*

Did I remember to sign my name?

Maybe the card got lost?

Maybe I sound like an insecure loser.

Elizabeth had all the goddamn control in this situation, and she knew it. I fucking hated it.

Sitting in my office that was bigger than my first apartment, I stared at the city, silently hating the fact that she wasn't in it. She was hundreds of miles away from me at the moment, and that fact had done nothing to quench my thirst for her. It only made my desire to see her that much stronger.

A man always wants what he can't have, I reminded myself.

But I knew deep down that it was more than that. Elizabeth wasn't some conquest I wanted to win. Yes, she challenged me with her sassy mouth and snarky responses, but that only made me want her more.

Plus, I'd meant it when I told her I wanted to kiss her again. I couldn't get her fucking lips or the taste of her tongue out of my head. Even my dick would wake up the second she popped into my mind. We were both clearly big fans of Elizabeth Lyons.

Could a man be blamed for wanting to get to know a woman better, for recognizing when someone special had entered his life? That was what I wanted, and so that was what I would get. I refused to take no for an answer from her. I'd warned her last night and again today in one of my emails.

Elizabeth sure as hell wasn't someone I was ready to let go of. I would have to take matters into my own hands. I'd make her see that I wanted more than just one night with her, and I'd convince her that she wanted the same thing.

heartless

episode 2

Elizabeth

When I walked into my office the next morning, the fragrance of roses overwhelmed my senses, forcing me to remember that I hadn't emailed Daniel to thank him. My day had been filled with back-to-back meetings, and I'd kept putting thanking him off until I finally just forgot before I left for home. As much as I wanted to ignore his gesture and whatever it meant, I couldn't be that rude.

I quickly turned on my computer screen and pulled up a blank email while wondering what exactly I should say to him.

TO: ALEXANDER, DANIEL

FROM: LYONS, ELIZABETH

SUBJECT: THANK YOU

I GOT SOME AMAZING FLOWERS YESTERDAY. ANY IDEA WHO THEY MIGHT BE FROM?

:)

It was simple and friendly but not overdone. When it came to Daniel, I wasn't sure at all how to handle him. I felt so out of practice.

By mid-afternoon, I'd already tackled five international conference calls, four in-person meetings, and one presentation for my bosses. I was beat. Stepping out of the elevator, I walked toward my office, but then I stopped dead in my tracks.

What the hell is he doing here?

Leaning over Barbara's desk, smiling and pointing at something in her hair, was fucking Daniel Alexander, all six feet three inches of him. Barbara glanced at her computer screen and said something to Daniel before glancing over her shoulder, her eyes meeting mine.

I gave her a look that warned her I'd be killing her later, and I started walking again.

"See, Daniel? Here she is. Right on time, like I told you."

Daniel stood there, staring at me, his face pleasant and his eyes filled with lust. Even though I'd banned men, I still recognized want filled eyes when I saw them.

"What are you doing here?" I tried to act angry, but inside, I was secretly thrilled. I never thought I'd see him again so soon.

"Nice to see you, too." He winked and gave me a smile.

"I'm sure it is. How did you get through security?"

We had a two-pronged security system on the lot. You had to pass through the initial gates just to park on the property, and then my actual building had its own security as well. Everyone had to be on a list, show ID, check in, wait to be called up, and then be escorted inside to the proper floor and office.

I glared at Barbara. "You let him in, didn't you?"

Traitor. I should fire her.

Her eyes widened. "He was already on the lot. I only let him upstairs."

"So, you were the worst offender then," I huffed. I turned my back to both of them before walking into my office and shutting the door, leaving Daniel standing outside of it.

If I were at my house, I would have slammed the door so hard that the whole wall would shake. But I couldn't behave like a fifteen-year-old girl in the office, so I'd settled for closing it—hard.

Stalking over to my desk, I plopped down, clearly frazzled by Daniel's arrival. My door opened, and Daniel's body appeared, my insides heating at the sight of it. He was something to look at all right, and boy, did I enjoy looking. I silently willed myself to stay strong.

"I see you got my flowers."

"I sent you an email, thanking you, this morning."

"I got it when I landed."

"Seriously, Daniel, what do you want? Why aren't you in your sucky part of the state right now?" I fired off anything my mind could think up that didn't involve kissing or naked body parts.

"My sucky part? My part of the state is way better than yours," he shot back.

"Then, you should go back there. I'm sure it misses you."

"You ignored my emails and voice mails. As of last night, you didn't say shit about the flowers. I told you I wanted to see you." He stalked over to my desk and pulled out a guest chair before unbuttoning his jacket. As he sat, it fell open, revealing a well-fit button shirt underneath.

"You didn't come down here because I'd ignored you. Be serious." I stole a glance at the roses sitting close by.

"I came here because I scheduled a meeting in Santa Monica tonight, but I came down early because you ignored me."

"You can't just show up here and expect my attention. Unlike you, apparently, I have actual work to do." I waved my hand toward a giant stack of unread scripts.

"No, you don't," he countered.

I bristled, my joy at seeing him quickly turning into something else. "Excuse me?"

"I checked your schedule with Barbara. You just have one meeting left, and then you're clear for the rest of the day."

I growled. I would be having a talk with Barbara about the information she chose to share with people who did not deserve to have such information. "I'm going to kill her or fire her. Which would be worse?" I cocked my head to the side.

"Firing would make her suffer more—unless you're really cruel in the murder, but you don't seem like the type." Daniel pushed out of the chair and stood, his large frame towering in front of me. "Come here," he demanded.

"No," I shot back.

"Elizabeth," he said my name with so much want that it lit a fire inside me. "Please get up and come here."

"What for?" I sounded like an ungrateful child.

"Because I flew out here to kiss you. I told you in my email that I needed to do it again. I meant it. I can't stop thinking about you."

"Try." I attempted to maintain control of my senses, but they were flying out the window with each word spilling off his tongue.

"I don't want to. Now, get up before I come over there and make you get up."

My jaw clenched as my mind debated which option would give me the most control. I didn't like being bossed around, but having it done by Daniel Alexander was sort of a turn-on. Pushing against the desk, I rolled away from the security of it and rose to my feet, waving my arm in his direction. "I'm up."

In the two seconds it took for me to say those words, he was in front of me, his body hulking. "I like kissing you," he said as one hand slipped under my skirt and grabbed my bare ass.

I gasped from the surprise movement, but I didn't pull away. The feel of his hand clutching and kneading my ass riled me up as heat spread between my thighs. I actually thought my body might melt into a puddle on the floor. His lips found mine, and my mouth instinctively opened to his, allowing his tongue to enter once again. Our lips opened and closed as my breathing grew heavier. His free hand gripped the back of my neck, holding me in place, as he panted against me, his mouth unable to get enough of mine.

He removed his grasp from my neck and reached for my free hand, leading it on top of the hard bulge in his pants. "Do you feel what you do to me?" he asked against my lips.

I stopped kissing him and pulled my hand away, feeling like an idiot, as my senses crashed down around me. The turn-on button suddenly switched off.

Am I supposed to be impressed with a hard-on? I mean, don't get me wrong, it felt impressive, but that's not what I meant.

"I make your dick hard? I'm sorry, but you guys get hard-ons if the wind blows across your pants the right way. That's not really a compliment."

"My dick doesn't behave like that."

"Excuse me?" I wiped my bottom lip and took a step away from him, wondering how seriously I should take him.

"It doesn't get hard on a whim. It's fickle. It sure as shit doesn't listen to me. But it likes you—a lot."

He glanced down at his pants, and my eyes followed.

"Do girls really buy your line of crap?" I tried to stay tough, but the size of his bulge made me want to drop to my knees and welcome it to my place of employment.

"They do. But I'm not lying to you, Elizabeth. My dick has a mind of its own. Right now, you're the only one it thinks about."

"You're an idiot." I started laughing and couldn't stop.

Who talks about his dick that way? Only a superficial, self-assured asshole would walk around, spouting crap about his dick having a mind of its own. But if I hated it so much, why the hell am I so damn tempted to test his theory?

Daniel walked toward me again, and I stood firm. He wrapped his arms around me and pulled me against him, my body pressing into his. As his muscles tightened, I lost myself in his touch. It was too easy to lose all focus in his presence.

I glanced up at his unshaven chiseled jaw, and I didn't know what came over me, but I kissed it. The rough stubble scraped against my lips like sandpaper, a feeling I'd never realized I enjoyed until this moment.

I licked at his chin before working my way down his neck and back up to his ear. "I think you should go," I whispered.

He laughed and gave me a full smile. "Not on your life."

His hand slipped up my skirt again, but this time, his fingers headed straight toward my most private area, and I jerked away, swatting at him.

"What's the matter?" he asked, completely unfazed.

I sucked in a breath and shook my head. "You can't just come here and manhandle me like you own me."

"I want you, Elizabeth."

"You just think you want me."

He stepped toward me, and I moved back, keeping my distance from his godlike features.

"No, I know I do. You want me, too. Don't deny it."

Oh, I'll try all right.

"I felt the heat coming off you." He smirked.

That was it.

Scowling, I practically came unglued. "You felt the heat coming off me? Are you serious with this? Who talks like that? This isn't some movie where you can waltz into my office, boss me around, and have your way with me."

Never mind that I'd allowed him to do exactly that. Now wasn't the time for logic.

He turned away before looking at me again, the expression on his face resembling embarrassment. "I'm not trying to be a dick, I swear," he half-apologized.

I almost believed him.

"Don't be mad at me." His head dipped as his eyes lowered to the floor.

"I'm not. I'm mad at me." I sucked in a breath before pointing at him and adding, "And you." I moved to sit back down behind my desk. "Who talks to women they just met like that? I barely know you, so you can't just say those things to me."

Truth be told, I was a little uncomfortable. It had been far too long since I had sex, much less been intimately touched by a man. I wasn't prepared for someone like Daniel.

"Most women like dirty talk." He moved to lean against the wall in my office, and he buttoned up his suit jacket.

"Well, I'm not most women."

"You can say that again." His eyes bored into mine as he licked his bottom lip.

Curse my fucking life if it didn't make me all hot and bothered again. I did not want to be turned on by him, but my brain was not factoring into this equation. Daniel forced everything inside me into sexual overdrive, and it pissed me off.

"Don't you have somewhere to be?" I asked.

He smiled and nodded. "Okay, Elizabeth. I'll leave you alone—for now."

"There is a God." I pretended not to care about anything he was doing or saying as I stood up from my desk and walked over to my office door. I opened it and watched him walk out at a snail's pace.

"This isn't over," he whispered against my ear before planting a soft kiss on my cheek.

Barbara surveyed our every move with watchful eyes.

"You keep saying that." I shut my door, so I wouldn't have to see him leave.

"I'll walk you down." Barbara's voice filtered through my closed door before doing what I assumed was, escort him off the premises.

Plopping down on my two-person couch, I closed my eyes and wondered what the hell I was going to do about this guy.

Daniel

I left Elizabeth's office with my virtual tail tucked between my legs. Her assistant, Barbara, was required to lead me off the property and to my car, so I intended on taking full advantage of the few minutes I had with her.

"So, Barbara..." I eyed her and watched as her cheeks turned rosy.

"Yes, Daniel?" she responded before punching the elevator down button.

"Do you think I scared her off?"

Her hip jutted to one side as she contemplated my question. "Honestly? I don't. You just need to be gentle with her. Elizabeth's had a rough time when it comes to relationships."

I found myself nodding along with her words. "I figured as much."

The elevator doors opened, and we stepped inside.

"This isn't a game for you, right? She isn't just some piece of ass you're trying to bang?"

Barbara's forwardness surprised me but only for a second. "No," I said, laughing at her choice of language.

"So, you don't want to have sex with her?"

I squinted my eyes, unsure of how to respond, when she spoke up again, "I'm just kidding, Daniel. But, really, don't hurt her. If this doesn't mean anything to you, then you need to walk away from her right now. She'll be fine, I promise, but not if you don't stop."

"I can't walk away anymore. Hell, I'm not sure I ever could." I thought back to waiting outside the bathroom for her. I'd tried to convince myself to walk away, knowing damn well that I couldn't.

The doors opened, and sunlight filled the space. I lowered my shades over my eyes and allowed Barbara to exit first before I pointed in the direction of my car.

"Why do you care so much?" she asked.

For the first time, I admitted, "'Cause I see something in her that I rarely see in women. No offense, Barbara." I clicked the unlock button on the key remote for my Jaguar rental.

She laughed. "None taken. What is it you think you see?"

"She's the total package, you know? Beauty and brains— not to mention, that fucking smart little mouth of hers." I practically drooled from just thinking about it.

"She is definitely all those things." Barbara's face lit up.

"Then, you understand why I can't let her get away from me, not without seeing."

"Seeing what?"

"Seeing if this could work. I'd never forgive myself if I didn't try."

"Did you even know she existed before the other night?"

I smiled. "I had no idea what I was missing before the other night."

"Oh God, Daniel. Don't mess this up."

"I don't plan on it, but I might need your help."

I reached out to shake her hand, and she pulled me in for a quick hug.

"You got it."

Elizabeth

Soft knocking interrupted my thoughts as the door creaked open. Barbara's long dark hair spilled across the doorframe as her face peeked inside.

"You alive in there?" she asked, her eyes searching for me behind my desk before landing on the couch. "There you are. I'm coming in."

I stayed quiet as she moved to sit next to me, plopping her feet up on the table before leaning back. "So," she started, "he's seriously good-looking."

"I'm aware," I breathed out.

"I think he likes you, like really likes you." Her head turned to face me, so I could look her in the eyes.

"He doesn't even know me. You can't like someone you don't know."

She huffed, "Fine. Then, I think he's interested in you, really interested in you."

"I don't care," I lied.

"Elizabeth." She paused. "I think your hoo-ha has been closed for business for way too long. It's officially killed you. If you weren't turned-on by that man who was just in your office, then you are officially dead inside. Death by vagina neglect. We should probably have a funeral."

I laughed and covered my face with my hands. "How do you come up with these things? My hoo-ha? Is that what they call it in the dirty South?"

"I didn't know what else to call it!"

She laughed out loud, and I giggled beside her.

"I'm not dead inside, trust me. That man has made me far too aware of how undead my lady parts are—not to mention, how badly they want him," I admitted with conflict in my voice.

"So then"—she looked up at me and batted her eyelashes like a love-struck teenager—"what are you gonna do about it?"

"Ignore it, and hope it goes away?" I batted my lashes back at her to show her how ridiculous she looked.

Her mouth fell open. "You absolutely will not." She sounded horrified.

"You're not the boss of me."

"This is all going to be okay, you know. I know you're scared."

Her words caused my stomach to twist into knots. She was absolutely right. I was more than scared. I was plain terrified.

"But I think he's worth the risk. Don't you?"

Yes. "I don't know. What if I'm just a challenge to him or something? What if none of it is real, and he just *thinks* he wants me? I can't go through something like that, not with someone like him." My admission spilled from my lips, surprising both myself and Barbara.

"I think it's more than that."

"How do you know?"

"Just trust me for once."

I leaned my head against her shoulder. "I always trust you."

I pulled my silver Audi to a stop in the underground parking of my beachfront condo. Living in Santa Monica never got old. I had an amazing view of the beach, and I could see the lights of the pier from my living room window. Beachside living was good, and I was blessed.

Once upstairs, I changed into a sports bra, tank top, and shorts before it got any later. I laced up my running shoes and stretched out my legs and arms, using my appliances for balance. I headed outside into the warm evening air, thankful for the ocean breeze. When I had the chance, I loved running down a bike path that stretched from Venice Beach all the way to Malibu.

I was determined to run my conflicted emotions for Daniel Alexander right out of my body. But that son of a bitch had proven more resilient than my feet pounding against the concrete because as I headed back forty minutes later, he was still firmly rooted in my mind with no intentions of leaving.

As I stopped to stretch after my run, a muscular frame caught my eye. A man was sitting on the concrete wall directly in front of my building. His head was in his hands, but I instantly recognized him. *How was it that his frame was already ingrained in my consciousness?*

Breathing hard, I stopped in front of him. "Stalking is illegal." *Was it?* "Or at least frowned upon in most states."

His eyes widened in surprise as they darted up to take me in. "Elizabeth," he stumbled, not sounding like the arrogant, confident guy I'd come to know. "I didn't know you'd be here, I swear."

"Are you sure my assistant didn't give you my address? She's given you everything else it seems." At this point, I'd put nothing past Barbara and her mission to get my lady parts in working order.

"I told you I had a meeting in Santa Monica tonight. I was just walking around, and I stopped to think."

He didn't look okay. His hair was frazzled, like he'd been pulling at it for hours, and his tie was loosened unevenly.

"Are you all right?"

"I'm so frustrated." He eyed me before turning away. "These businessmen wanted to talk to me about investing in this brilliant fucking idea they have, but they don't want to hear how they can make it better. Creative types always think they're right, that their ideas are the only and best way."

I moved to sit down next to him, torn between wanting to comfort him and wanting to keep my distance. "Tell me what happened."

He stared off at the ocean instead of at me. "Everyone wants a piece of my money, right? You know how that is."

I did know how it was but not to the level that he did.

"I get proposals to invest in start-ups all the time. This one…" His head shook as he turned to look at me. "This one is really brilliant, even James thought so."

"Who's James?" I breathed out, my heartbeat still trying to return to normal after my run.

"Sorry. He's my business partner. Anyway, it's so innovative, and I love the concept, but I can see the flaws in it. I pointed them out and told them how to fix it, but they were so pigheaded." He raked his fingers through his hair before glancing up at me.

"People don't like being told they're wrong or that their innovative ideas aren't innovative enough," I said, not telling him anything he didn't already know.

"It was a risk to begin with going into it, and I knew that. The lead guy on the project is a buddy of mine, which always makes shit weird, but he knows that I know what I'm talking about."

"So, what has you pissed off more? The fact that they won't listen or that *he* won't?" I scooted my body a little closer to his and placed my hand on his thigh to calm and comfort him.

He tilted his head and rested it against my shoulder.

I tensed briefly before forcing myself to relax. "I'm sorry if I stink. I've been running."

"I noticed. You don't stink. You smell like you," he said, not moving his head.

"Do you want to come upstairs? My condo is right here. Sounds like you could use a beer."

What the hell was I thinking? A few hours ago, I'd wanted to maintain my distance from this guy, and now, I was inviting him into my most personal space. I considered myself a strong woman, but this was going too far, even for me.

"You know if I come upstairs, we're not just going to talk." He nudged against me.

"What do you mean?" I played stupid.

"You let me inside your place, and I'm going to try to have sex with you, Elizabeth."

I nodded before standing up and reaching out my hand. "I know, Daniel. I know."

He sucked in a long, deep breath as I waited, my hand empty. "I probably shouldn't." His words caused me to drop my hand to my side.

Did he just tell me no?

I was willing to chip away at the cement wall that I had not only wanted, but also helped to erect eight years ago. Now, I wanted to put every slightly moved brick back in its rightful place around my heart.

"I should go then."

I turned to walk away from him when his hand reached out and grabbed mine. Turning back around to face him, I waited for him to say something. His silence sliced through my ego as he slowly let go of my hand. I couldn't reach the entrance of my building quickly enough as I turned to go. I felt so stupid.

"Elizabeth?" His voice stopped me cold.

"What?" I asked before glancing back at him .

He waved me over. "I forgot to give this to you earlier."

I watched as he pulled a plain white envelope from his jacket pocket and held it in the air.

"What is this?" I looked at it before grabbing it.

"Open it."

I tore through the top and noticed a crisp one-hundred-dollar bill inside. "What is this for?"

"What can I say?" He paused. "You were right. You won the bet."

I pulled my head back and furrowed my forehead. "What bet?"

"You bet me a hundred bucks that one of my friends with benefits wanted more, remember?"

"I remember." A sick feeling washed through me. "So, how did you prove me right?" *God, I didn't want to know the*

71

answer to this question if it involved him having sex with someone who wasn't me.

Daniel rose to his feet, his frame towering over mine. "I broke off my prior commitments, and one of the girls had a meltdown, a fucking meltdown." He sounded so surprised. "She called me heartless and then basically said all the same stuff that you did, pretty much word for fucking word. It was brutal."

He continued to talk, but my ears had stopped listening after hearing that he'd broken off his "*prior commitments.*"

"You stopped seeing your friends with benefits? When?"

"The night I met you." He thumbed my chin and planted a kiss on my cheek before turning his body away.

"You sure you don't want to come up?" I asked again as a rush of emotions soared through me.

"Not tonight," he said before walking away.

Elizabeth

Maneuvering my car into my assigned parking space at work, I tried to rid my head of thoughts of Daniel when I should have been thinking about my nine a.m. meeting.

Apparently, he had flown back to San Francisco last night after our encounter. I wasn't sure why exactly, but I'd half-expected to see him again or at least hear from him before he'd headed back to his part of the state. Maybe it was more of what I'd wanted than what I'd expected. Disappointment coursed through me, and that only proved to fuel both my intrigue and my annoyance.

Admitting to myself, if no one else, that Daniel Alexander happened to be growing on me was something I was reluctant to do, especially after last night. Granted, it could have been worse, I imagined. He could have come into my place, screwed me senseless, and then left without a word.

Which would be worse—rejection or being dismissed?

Ugh.

Eight years alone was a long enough time to get used to the idea of being single. All it had taken was one night at a stupid mixer I never wanted to attend in the first place to make me want to throw it all away.

Walking into my office, I flipped on the light switch and smiled at the roses on my desk. Shaking my head to rid it of all thoughts of him, I sat down and tried to focus on my upcoming meeting.

My cell phone pinged, and I looked down to see a text message from an unknown number.

> *Back in my sucky part of the state. It would be far less sucky if you were here with me. I'm sorry about last night.*

Heat coursed through my body, and I felt my cheeks flush. I wondered how he'd gotten my cell phone number, but then I glared out my door at my assistant's empty chair.

Who is this? Do I know you?

I giggled as I pressed the Send button. I was enjoying this flirtation, or whatever the hell it was, a little too much.

Can I call you? Or are you busy?

Gripping my phone, I stared at his words. *I can do this*, I thought, trying to convince myself. It would be okay.

You can call.

My cell phone vibrated almost immediately. "Hello?" I practically sang into the receiver.

"Miss Lyons." His deep voice sounded even sexier through the phone.

"How did you get my number?" I cut to the chase.

He huffed out a quick laugh. "I'm not giving up my sources."

"I think it's a short list. I know who to blame."

"Don't be mad."

"I'm not," I admitted as I focused on a picture of the studio in 1942 hanging on my wall.

"I'm sorry I left like that."

"I don't know what you're talking about."

Deny.

Deny.

Deny.

"So stubborn." His voice sounded smooth and relaxed, almost like he was in bed.

"What can I say? You bring out the best in me."

"Elizabeth," he said my name, and I literally felt my body tingle. "I wasn't in a good place last night. If I had followed you upstairs to your place, it would have ended badly."

74

"Why's that?" That easily, my anger was replaced by want.

"Because I was mad. I was frustrated, and I needed to figure out how to fix the shitstorm of a meeting I'd just walked out of. James was going to be pissed at me for blowing it, and I needed to brainstorm."

"You didn't tell me you'd walked out."

"I walked out."

"Smart-ass." Every time he exhaled into the phone, I'd inhale, convincing myself that I was breathing in his air. "All I wanted to do was let you vent. I could have helped. I just wanted to talk."

"Well, I wouldn't have just wanted to talk to you, okay? We would have gone to your place, and I would have been dying to get you naked. I want you, Elizabeth. When I finally do get you, it's not going to be because I had a shitty day at the office, and you're feeling sorry for me."

"Let's get one thing clear." My voice escalated as agitation bloomed. "I do not feel sorry for you, okay?"

The phone stayed silent, and I pulled it away from my ear to make sure the call hadn't disconnected.

"Okay?" I asked again.

"Okay." His voice sounded soft, and I wanted to curl up next to his body and envelop him. "So, do you forgive me?"

"Yes."

"And we're okay?"

"Sure." I shrugged, wondering what that even meant.

"Good. Then, I want to see you again. I don't care if I have to come down there every week or every day. You will give this a shot, and I'll make up for last night."

"Give what a shot exactly?" I questioned, already knowing the answer but desperately wanting to hear him say it.

"Us."

"There is no us," I responded, sounding like a brat.

"We've started something here. Fight it all you want, but it's already happening, and you know it."

I sighed and allowed the silence that followed to speak for me.

"Listen to me," his voice started again. "I know you're scared. I don't pretend to know why, but I want to know. Someday, I hope you'll tell me."

"Why would I tell you anything?" I whispered as my mind replayed my dad leaving and Ben cheating, coupled with Daniel denying me last night.

"Eventually—and by eventually, I mean, really, really soon—" He paused, and I held my breath as I waited for him to finish. "I'm going to be your boyfriend. Although, I'm really more of a man, don't you think? Soon, I'm going to be your *manfriend*, and you're going to trust me and fall head over heels in love with me."

I laughed hard. "You're hilarious."

"I'm serious."

"Delusional much?"

"Not often."

"I have to go." I shifted in my chair, causing it to roll to the side.

"Talk to you later, babe. Have a good day." He hung up before I could respond.

My thoughts recycled his words over and over until I felt almost dizzy from them.

Daniel

Subtlety had never been my strong suit. Being an aggressive businessman often spilled over into other aspects of my life, if I allowed it. When I saw something I wanted, I would go after it with vigor.

The minute Elizabeth had walked away last night, I'd cursed myself for blowing it with her, and I'd vowed to make it right. I knew that not going upstairs with her was the right thing to do, but I hadn't even fucking said a thing about it to her. I'd let her walk away, thinking that I wasn't interested. I'd make sure she knew that was the furthest thing from the truth.

I was interested.

I was all in.

A woman like Elizabeth wouldn't stay single for long, and for the life of me, I had no fucking idea why she still was. I assumed it had to be on her end because there was no way that guys wouldn't hit on her every time she left the house. She was gorgeous, and that wasn't even the half of it.

Then again, we were talking about men in Los Angeles, and they were a different breed altogether—pussies, as I liked to call them, or pretty boys who cared more about their own wardrobe and hairstyle than any real man should. Most of them would have a hard time handling a successful woman like Elizabeth.

It was a good thing I wasn't most men.

The sound of knuckles rapped on my door three times before it swung open without saying a word. I didn't even have to look up from my computer to know who it was.

"James."

"Daniel," he said before moving over to the full-sized couch and spreading out.

"Don't you have work to do?" I tried to sound authoritative, but he only laughed.

James and I had been buddies since our freshman year at Stanford. We had been assigned to the same dormitory on the same floor, but we weren't roommates. After a few too many beers one night, we'd realized that we were cut from the same cloth, as my mother would say. We had both been raised in affluent families, but we were determined to make names for ourselves without any help from our parents. It was a pretty typical story, if you asked me, but the difference between James and every other spoiled rich brat I'd met throughout my life until then was…he'd actually meant it.

When it came to the girls at our college, we were each other's perfect wingman. My dark hair contrasted James's blond locks, and girls were usually attracted to one of us immediately, depending on their hair-color preference. It was that easy.

He was smart as hell, too, so I'd liked him immediately. When we'd collaborated on our first business venture to develop a new cell phone app, he'd willingly taken a backseat to me. He'd said that when it came to the meetings and convincing people to take a risk on a couple of nineteen-year-old kids, I had an ability to charm money out of rich guys' wallets better than anyone he'd ever known. He'd included his dad in that compliment.

In that moment, I'd trusted him not to fuck me over, and he'd been working for me ever since—although it was usually in a business-partner capacity. There wasn't a single venture or business move I'd make that didn't involve James.

"How was LA?" he asked between yawns.

"Warm."

"Isn't it always?"

I looked up at him as his eyes closed, and I searched for something on my desk to throw at his head. Settling on a pen, I chucked it across the room, and it landed square on his forehead with a *dink* sound.

Nailed it.

"Ow! Fucker!" He sat up, rubbing the red mark with his hand.

"Sleep in your own office. What do you want?" I knew exactly what he wanted.

James was the only person in the world who knew almost everything about me. There was very little I kept hidden from him.

"How was the Santa Monica meeting? Are we in or what?"

I groaned. "It's a pretty groundbreaking idea."

"Then, what's the problem? Why the groan?"

"There's a flaw in their basic system. It's a minor issue, but it's definitely a deal-breaker. I asked them to send me their business proposal and projections, so I could look them over one more time." I left out the part where I'd walked out of the meeting as if my ass were on fire.

"Want me to check it out as well?"

"I do actually." I nodded. "As soon as I get it, I'll forward it to you."

"Sounds good," he answered.

He made no moves to get off my couch. I waited for the reason he'd really barged in, but he remained silent.

"Oh, for fuck's sake, just ask already." I stared at my best friend and tried to hide the smile forming on my lips.

He leaned back and howled out a laugh toward the ceiling. "Did you see Elizabeth or what?"

"Of course I fucking saw her. I told you I was going to."

"And?" He waited.

"To be honest, I thought she was going to kick my ass. She scares the crap out of me sometimes."

He howled again.

"Dude, stop howling. Serena's going to think you're dying, and she'll come rushing in here to save you."

Serena was my assistant—my very-married, very-mom-of-three assistant. It had been a requirement of mine to hire someone I wouldn't be tempted to fuck when we worked late hours. I never fucked my employees, but sometimes, shit happened. So, I had taken that extra layer of precaution and made sure my assistant was not only *not* my type, but also not available. I never touched married women—ever.

"So, she didn't get the roses?"

"Oh, she got them all right. They were sitting on her fucking desk when I walked into her office."

"Ah, hell. This is great." He continued laughing at my expense.

"Fuck off." I was half-tempted to throw another pen at his head to get him to shut up.

"When do I get to meet her?" He leaned forward as he clapped his hands together and started rubbing them back and forth as if he were concocting an evil scheme.

I snarled, "Never."

He threw his hands up in surrender. "Now, you know what it's like not to have every girl fall at your feet. Can't blame me for thinking that shit is funny."

I didn't. I completely understood, but that didn't mean I liked it. "I like her."

"I know."

"A lot," I added for emphasis.

"I'm aware."

"So, what do I do?"

"Send more roses," he said with another guttural laugh.

"I already did."

"Fuck, Daniel. I was joking."

"Either be helpful, or get the fuck out." I glared at him, but it was no use. Trying to stay mad at James was like trying to stay mad at a puppy. It just wasn't possible.

"Don't get pissy. Let me have my fun. I've never seen you like this before, all riled up over a girl."

"Well, enjoy it while it lasts."

"You plan on getting over her soon?"

"Fuck no. I plan on getting under her—among other things." I smirked.

6

Elizabeth

Barbara knocked on my open office door before waltzing in, carrying another vase spilling over with all white roses.

"My God," my voice breathed out at the sight of them.

I wasn't sure what it was about white roses, but when the first bouquet from Daniel had arrived, I had decided that they were my new favorite flower. I had also agreed that any lingering anger from the night before was officially gone as of this moment. It'd all stemmed from my ego and pride anyway.

"Seriously, Elizabeth, if you don't marry this man, can I?" She placed the vase on top of the drawer of files behind my desk.

Spinning my chair around, I reached for the card, wondering what it would say this time.

ALL I SEE IS YOU.

I swooned, out loud, before handing the card to Barbara to read.

"You should probably at least call him this time to thank him."

"You're so helpful."

"I'm here all week." She winked and closed my office door, leaving me alone.

It was her subtle way of telling me what to do.

Staring at my cell phone, I debated between sending him a text or calling him. Texting seemed too impersonal at this point, but after our phone call this morning, I wasn't sure how much more of his words I could take hearing.

Fuck it.

I dialed his cell phone number and held my breath with each ring.

"Elizabeth," he breathed my name into the phone.

Part of me melted into my chair. "Thank you for the roses, Daniel."

He laughed slightly. "I'm impressed."

"Why's that?"

"You actually called me the day you got them this time. Unless…" He stopped mid-thought.

"Unless what?"

"Unless you only called me so that I wouldn't show up at your work again. Are you trying to keep me away from you?"

It was my turn to laugh. "No," I admitted honestly.

"Good. Have dinner with me tonight then," he said.

My breath caught in my throat. "Tonight? Where?" I started looking at the door as if he'd bust through it again at any moment.

"At The Penthouse."

"In The Huntley Hotel?" I wondered.

"You're familiar with it?" he asked, his tone delightfully surprised.

"Of course."

The Penthouse was one of my favorite restaurants to entertain in Santa Monica. It was eighteen stories up and had the most incredible view of the coastline on one side and the city on the other. Not to mention, the food and atmosphere were amazing.

"It's beautiful there," I added.

"It's a date. I'll pick you up at seven."

I sucked in a quick breath. "Actually, I'll just meet you there. You know I live only a few blocks away. It will just be easier." After last night, I wasn't ready for any more home-related expectations.

"Have it your way." He didn't fight me on it, which surprised me. "See you tonight."

He ended the call.

Oh my gosh, I had just agreed to a real-life date with someone and not just any someone—him.

Please don't break my heart. Please don't break my heart, I silently prayed to the gods above, hoping like hell they were listening.

I stepped into the lobby of the hotel, my red dress inching higher with each stride. Grabbing the bottom of it, I gave it one final tug, willing it to stay put against my thighs. He came into view, and he looked incredible in navy blue suit pants, a lighter blue shirt and a matching navy tie. The man was simply stunning to look at, and boy did I enjoy looking.

Watching his face light up at the sight of me made me feel sexy and wanted—two things I hadn't cared about in so long. As we walked toward each other, his right hand moved from behind his back, and a single long-stemmed white rose appeared.

"For you." He handed it to me before bending down and sweeping me into his arms in a tight hug. "You look beautiful."

My cheeks warmed with the combination of being touched by him and by his compliment. "Thank you. You look very nice yourself." I sniffed at the rose, loving that this was quickly becoming our thing.

We have a thing.
WE HAVE A THING!
Deep breaths, Elizabeth.

Daniel extended a hand toward the hotel elevator. "Shall we?"

I moved toward them, his hand resting firmly on my lower back.

We reached the eighteenth floor and stepped out into a plethora of candlelight.

A hostess immediately greeted us upon our exit. "Reservations?"

"Alexander, for two," Daniel said.

She smiled. "Right this way, Mr. Alexander."

We followed as she led us around the enormous bar and toward the part of the restaurant that faced the coastline. Although, in the dark, we couldn't see it.

The table sat in the corner, away from other people, and I realized that Daniel had most likely requested that arrangement, so we could have some sense of privacy. I scooted into the comfortable bench seat, and Daniel sat across from me in a baby-blue plush chair.

I started to laugh.

"Why are you laughing at me?" He veered forward, his face glowing in the candlelight.

"Because you're so manly, but that chair is so girlie. You look ridiculous, sitting in it." I continued to giggle.

He leaned back. "You think I'm manly, huh?"

"Compared to the chair," I fired back.

"My Elizabeth, always so sassy."

I swooned—silently and to myself, but I still did it.

"I'm sorry again about last night."

"I'm over it. Let's not talk about it anymore."

I wanted to be done with it. He'd apologized, and I'd forgiven him. It was time to move on.

"You're incredible, you know that?" he complimented.

"You're all right," I teased.

Our waitress appeared, and I was thankful for the break in the awkwardness.

"Good evening. My name's Heather, and I'll be your waitress tonight. Can I start you off with something to drink?"

Daniel nodded at me, and I glanced at the wine menu. "I'll take a glass of your dry Riesling."

"Make it a bottle," he interjected.

Heather smiled at him. She was charmed by the sight of him, the same way I had been. Only, it had taken her all of two seconds.

"Of course. Would you like to hear our specials?"

"Just the wine for now. Thanks." He dismissed her. It wasn't rude, but it wasn't overly friendly either.

I watched as Heather's smile dropped a little before she turned away.

Daniel

Elizabeth looked absolutely gorgeous. I couldn't stop staring at her face, her eyes, her mouth, and her ass when she'd walked in front of me. Everything about this woman called to me. Hell, I'd already flown out to see her twice in as many days. I might need an intervention.

"So, Elizabeth," I started, hoping she'd let me in on some of her mystery tonight.

"So, Daniel," she countered before continuing, "are you going to make this sort of thing a habit?"

"What sort of thing?" I asked playfully.

Her head tilted to one side, allowing her long hair to spill down across her shoulder. With her bare neck revealed, I instantly hardened. I wanted to slide next to her and feast on her skin. *Fuck dinner. I had everything I needed sitting across from me.*

"Flying out here to see me," her voice said.

I blinked twice to regain focus. "I'm planning on it, yes. Is that going to be a problem?" *Please fucking say no.*

She sighed, and I reached across the table for her hand.

"I don't think so, but how can you afford to do that with your job?"

I stifled a laugh. "It's only an hour flight, so it's not like I'm losing much of my day when I'm in the air. Also, I can work from Southern California just as effectively as I can from my office up north." Squeezing her hand for a moment, I added, "Well, almost as effectively. You've been a bit of a distraction lately."

"Me? You're the distraction, and I haven't even had to leave my office. You bring the distraction to me."

She half-smiled, and I wanted to kiss the edges of her mouth.

"Do you want me to stop?"

Her eyes skirted away from mine as she glanced at our hands. "No."

"Good. I wouldn't have listened anyway. To be honest, I think we have the perfect situation here." My thumb lazily circled hers.

"How so?"

"Well, for starters, we don't live anywhere near each other," I practically shouted at her like an excited five-year-old.

"I think we've established that already. Why is that a good thing?"

"Well, contrary to what you think, I really do work hard and long hours. I get home late all the time, and I'm up early. I know you are, too. Neither of us has time for a demanding relationship, not that I think you'd ever be demanding. You're too damn independent." Her lips started to frown, and I quickly recovered. "That's a good thing. I fucking love that about you." I watched as her lips tilted up into a slight grin. "As I was saying, I think that us being long distance is the perfect way for you to take baby steps, which I'm assuming you need to do, before we go all in. And trust me, babe, we're going all in."

"Are you always this overly confident, bossy, and demanding?"

"Only when I know I'm right." I smirked before bringing her hand to my lips.

"So, all the time then," she teased.

"See? You're the perfect girlfriend already." The word effortlessly slipped off my tongue. I hadn't had a real girlfriend in years, but I wanted this. I wanted her.

Heather reappeared at that moment with our bottle of wine and two glasses, and all I wanted her to do was leave again. We placed our order, and I informed her we weren't in a rush.

"Will you answer me something?" I asked with slight apprehension.

"Sure."

She looked tentative, but I was determined to convince her that she could trust me.

"Why are you so hesitant when it comes to me?"

"It's not just you." She sipped her wine.

"Then, what is it?"

"I don't really date anymore. I kind of swore off men awhile back." Her eyes averted mine as she stared past me.

"So, you only date girls now?" I tried to break the tension.

She laughed. "Oh, yeah. I'm sure dating a chick would be far less dramatic." Her expression shifted.

"Tell me what happened. Please." I looked into her brown eyes and saw the hurt in them.

She was so reluctant about sharing anything personal with me, and it fucking killed me. I wanted her to trust me.

"Elizabeth, I know that someone hurt you, but that someone wasn't me."

And it never will be, I promised myself.

"I know that. It's so stupid." She shrugged one shoulder. "I mean, it happened eight years ago."

"But you're still holding on to it?" I honestly wondered.

"Not in the way you're thinking. It just affected the way I chose to live my life."

"In what way?" Now, we were getting somewhere.

"When it came to work and men."

Her eyes stared through me. They willed me to challenge her. She wanted to let this out. I could tell. I just had to push her to do it.

"This is like pulling teeth, Elizabeth. Just tell me what happened."

"Fine." Her tone was clipped. "My ex cheated on me with my roommate. He told me it was all my fault that he did it, and that's the gist of it."

My eyes narrowed in both confusion and anger. That couldn't possibly be the whole story because it didn't fucking add up.

What kind of asshole would cheat on her and tell her it was her fault?

A young one.

"How was him cheating on you your fault? I'd love to hear how he explained that one."

She sucked her bottom lip into her mouth, and my eyes zeroed in on it. The move momentarily stopped my brain from working and sent all my blood flowing south, but I forced myself to remain in my seat.

"He said that I was too focused on what I wanted for my future. I didn't give him enough attention because my dreams were too big. And no guy would ever want someone like me because I wanted too much for myself."

I couldn't listen to another word without wanting to smash something. "What kind of insecure piece of shit doesn't want his girlfriend to be successful?"

"That's what I said!" Her voice became animated at this point. "But he said that guys wanted their women to take care of them and support their goals, not have goals of their own. He said that all guys thought that way, not just him. And he acted like he was doing me a favor by telling me, like he was clueing me in on some giant secret in the book of men."

I shook my head back and forth so hard that I thought it might fall off my fucking shoulders. "I am so sorry that happened to you." Anger pulsed through every inch of my body. I could feel it seething through my veins like blood.

Pushing out of my chair, I rose to my feet and sucked in three deep breaths before sliding into the bench seat next to her. Wrapping my arms around her, I pulled her against me and kissed her forehead. My heart pounded against my chest. It wasn't because of the woman in my arms—although, that would have been enough. It was because my fucking adrenaline was pumping so hard. This guy had done a number on her, and I understood now why she had been so guarded.

What girl wouldn't be after experiencing that?

I looked down at her and reached for her chin, tilting it up with my fingertips, before pressing my lips against hers. If I had the power to kiss away all the bullshit she had been told in her life, I wished for it to work now.

My tongue swept across her bottom lip before begging for entry into her mouth. She parted her lips, and the taste of sweet wine was on her tongue. We kissed for a few seconds more before I slowly pulled away from her and planted a soft peck on her cheek.

Elizabeth

Sweet baby Jesus. If I'd known that telling Daniel that story would get me rewarded so sweetly, I might have shared it with him the night we first met.

No, I wouldn't have.

"Are you okay?" I asked.

I couldn't pretend not to notice the way his chest was inflating and deflating quicker than normal and that his jaw had been clenched since he sat back down on his side of the table.

"Me? I'm fine. What about you? You've been living with that shit in your head for how many years?" His tone was angry as he reached for the bread that had arrived shortly after the wine.

"Eight. Are you mad at me?"

His eyes widened in surprise. "At you? Why would I be mad at you?" His teeth ripped through a piece of the bread. "I'm mad at the dickhead who said that to you, the guy who put that in your head and allowed you to believe it."

"So, you don't think it's true? Guys don't really want that?"

It would take a lot more than one conversation to erase eight years of being brainwashed.

His light eyes met mine as he spoke, "Some guys want that, yes, but not me."

"Why not you?"

"Because I want you."

I huffed out a quick laugh. "Be serious."

"I am."

"Then, tell me why."

"It doesn't appeal to me. Listen, Elizabeth, some guys want their wives to stay at home, take care of the kids, have dinner ready every night, and basically, provide for their families."

I nodded my head, familiar with the wives of the executives at my office. Almost all of them were stay-at-home moms. That was a fact that had only fueled my belief that Ben was right.

"I've never wanted that," he continued.

I felt almost blessed with the truths he was about to share with me.

"That's why I think it's been so hard for me to find someone. I don't want the woman who has no ambitions of her own. I don't mind taking care of and providing for my family, but there's something innately attractive about a woman who makes shit happen."

His eyes closed for a moment before reopening. "You know, maybe it was because my mom stayed home while my dad worked. Sure, she volunteered at my school, and she was on quite a few charitable committees, but none of that shit paid her any money. While she was content and felt accomplished for a bit, she eventually wanted more—something for herself, something she earned. You know what I mean?"

I hummed out a yes in understanding.

"But she was over forty by then, and I watched as she searched to find her place in a world that wasn't made for a woman with no experience in the workforce. She eventually gave up her search and continued doing what she had always done, but I could tell she wasn't really happy. So, I offered her a job."

A smile spread across my face. "You did? Doing what?"

I finished off my glass of wine, and he filled it up.

"I started her off as the receptionist in my first company, but that didn't really work out well. To be honest, my mom is a bit of a snob. She answered all the phones, and she would get a lot of calls, way more than I'd ever realized, asking for charitable contributions. So, she convinced me that I needed someone to oversee the charities I donated to, and she helped me start up my own organization. It was the perfect fit."

"That's fantastic. I bet she loves handling that stuff for you."

"She does. Plus, she likes feeling like she can still tell me what to do sometimes, and I humor her."

Heather appeared with our food. It smelled amazing, but I wanted her to leave because this conversation was doing more for me personally than anything had in years.

When our waitress disappeared, I started right where we'd left off. "You're a good son."

"Even if that didn't happen with my mom, I don't think I could be happy with someone who didn't want to have her own thing." He took a man-sized bite of pasta.

"Really?" I felt my expression soften as my heart started to lighten its load.

"Oh God, this is really good." He stabbed at his plate with his fork before directing it toward me.

I leaned forward, taking the pasta in my mouth, and I moaned. "Holy smokes. Delicious."

He raised his eyebrows in response and continued, "I respect ambition, Elizabeth—not that I don't respect women who want to stay at home with their families because I do. That's hard work, and I'm not trying to diminish that *at all*," he emphasized. "But when it comes to me and the qualities that I'm attracted to, I look for that inner drive in a woman."

His hand balled into a fist, and he placed it over his heart. "When I look at you, I see that fire. Maybe I respect it so much just because I can relate to it. I don't know, but I do know that I want someone who gets what I'm going through every day. I want someone who knows how to build me up and make me a better man. Because that's exactly what I want to do for her."

My heart swelled inside my chest with his confession. I nodded my head so vigorously along with everything he said that I was certain I looked like a bobblehead doll. My eyes started to water.

"Oh, jeez, babe. Don't cry."

I waved him away. "I'm fine really. That's just the most…" I paused as I wiped away the few tears that had escaped.

"You're amazing. I would never have thought that you would be like this."

"Because you're ambitious and judgy," he teased.

"Only because you're arrogant and annoying."

"Touché," he said with a cocky smirk. "I knew I'd have you, Elizabeth. I just didn't know it would be so soon."

I admitted, "Me either."

"To which part?" He cocked his head to the side, and his hair moved slightly with it.

"I didn't think you'd get to me this quickly."

"But you knew I'd eventually get to you?"

"Of course I fucking knew."

"No one hotter…no one has ever been hotter than you are right now."

"I kind of want to climb over this table and have my way with you." I toyed with him, taking our flirtation to the next level.

He looked all around him before yelling, "Check, please!"

"I was kidding!" I swatted at his arm. *I was so not kidding.*

Daniel

"Don't forget this." I reached for the single white rose and handed it to her.

"I wasn't planning on it," she smiled before holding it with care.

With dinner over, I was torn between getting back on the plane or going to Elizabeth's place, if she'd have me. I didn't want her to think I was rejecting her in any way, but I had a six a.m. phone call, and I still needed to prepare for it. Girls tended to be touchy when they felt denied in any aspect, and I definitely didn't need that after last night's unplanned fiasco.

I started to call my driver before I turned toward her. "Do you want to call it a night?"

"Do you?"

Shit. After my idiocy last night, I needed to take control but also tread carefully. "I want to come over."

Her soft brown eyes widened. "To my place?"

"Yes, Elizabeth, to your place." My hands circled her waist and pulled her tightly against me.

"Okay."

She smiled up at me, and I knew that tonight was going better than we both had expected.

"But I have to warn you that I can't stay long. I have a six a.m. call."

"Six? That sucks. Overseas?"

She understood. Of course she fucking understood. She dealt with this sort of thing in her job, too.

"Rome. It's the only time we could get everyone's schedules to work. Sucks for me, but I can take the call from home."

"Ah, lucky." She smacked my shoulder.

"You don't ever take calls from home?"

She shook her head. "Nah. It's just easier to take them from the office. Plus, I like being there when no one else is. There's a quiet that doesn't exist at any other time. It's so peaceful."

I knew exactly what she meant. It was those hours early in the morning or late at night when the rest of the staff was long gone.

"I get some of my best work done during those times."

"Me, too. Come on. I'm parked on the street." Her ass swayed as she walked.

I knew being at her house meant there was no way in hell I'd be flying home tonight. I could try to convince myself that I would leave after having her, but I knew better.

"Elizabeth? Elizabeth Lyons!" A male voice that I recognized filtered through the night air.

I turned around, searching for its location.

"Holy shit! Daniel Alexander, too? What are the odds?"

I watched as Ben Anders jogged to catch up to us.

Elizabeth's grip on my arm tightened, and her entire body tensed next to mine. "You two know each other?" she whispered toward me.

"How do you two know each other?" I asked her at the same exact time.

10
Elizabeth

My eyes immediately met Daniel's as panic seared through me.

How had I avoided seeing Ben for the last eight years, but on one of the best nights of my life, he not only shows up, but he also knows my…he knows Daniel?

Ben's eyes flashed between my body and Daniel's, and his brows furrowed, his face holding tension I didn't recognize. He extended his arm to shake Daniel's hand, and Daniel reluctantly grabbed it.

"How do you guys know each other?" Daniel's question hung in the air like a guillotine waiting to drop.

"Elizabeth and I used to——" Ben started to say.

I stopped him, "We knew each other once, but that was a long time ago. We don't know one another at all anymore, not that we ever really did."

"Don't be like that, Elizabeth," Ben said, his tongue drawing out my name, slow and meaningful, as he shifted his weight between his feet.

His brown hair had started to thin, and part of me loved the fact that he was already going bald.

Karma, I thought to myself, *it's nice to see you.*

"Uh…" I stuttered, hating that I was forced to see him right now. I couldn't stand the way my name sounded coming from his lips. "Don't say my name like that, and don't tell me what to do."

Daniel's grip on my elbow alerted me to the fact that I was making a scene.

I turned to him, apologetic and embarrassed. "I'm sorry."

"Don't be. Are you okay?" Daniel asked.

I shook my head, my feelings splayed out across the cement like someone had driven over them like roadkill.

Ben stepped between Daniel and me, forcing unwanted space between us. "Daniel, may I please speak to Elizabeth alone for a moment?"

My mouth fell slightly ajar with his words. "We don't need to speak *alone*," I spit, infuriated at his choice of wording. "I don't need to speak to you at all."

"Looks like she doesn't want to talk to you, bud," Daniel spoke with authority, his chest puffing out, as he pulled me back toward him.

Ben's eyes pleaded with mine. "Please…please just let me talk to you for two minutes."

He placed his hands together in prayer pose and I sucked in a breath, wondering what could possibly be so important that he would beg me like this. I reluctantly agreed, "Fine. Two minutes."

He led me far enough away from Daniel so that he couldn't hear our conversation, but I was still close enough where he could keep a watchful eye on us.

And watch he did.

"What are you doing with Daniel Alexander, Elizabeth?" Ben asked.

"Is that really what you wanted to ask me?"

"Elizabeth, listen to me." His words rang with desperation. "I need to know what you're doing with him?"

"How's Kim?" I asked, pulling my virtual gloves off.

"Who? Who's Kim?" His face crinkled.

Who is Kim?

WHO IS KIM?

Has he seriously forgotten her name?

I didn't care how many years it had been. That name should have been tattooed on his fucking tongue or engraved on his memory when it came to me. I sure as hell related her name with his whenever he was brought up.

"You're a pig."

Recognition dawned on his face. "I haven't seen her since college. But, Elizabeth, why was Daniel holding your hand?" He was clearly determined not to stray from this singular topic.

"My personal life is none of your business."

"Yours might not be, but his is."

"How do you figure?" I asked, my tone more than simply annoyed.

"Because he's dating my sister."

"Jenny?" I asked.

His older sister's face filtered into my mind. It had been a long time since I last saw her, but it didn't add up. I couldn't see the Jenny I remembered with someone like Daniel.

"No, not Jenny. Kate," Ben corrected.

That made more sense simply based on looks. Kate had always been really beautiful, and she was two years younger than we were. But she wasn't at all motivated or particularly intelligent, if I recalled correctly.

Then, his words hit me all at once. He didn't say they used to date. He said they *were* dating—as in present tense.

Currently.

Now.

"What do you mean, he's dating your sister?" I asked, hoping he would correct me.

He only shrugged and took a tentative step toward me. "They've been dating on and off for years. Katie's completely in love with him. She adores Daniel. What I don't understand is, why are you here with him?"

This could not be happening. Daniel had told me he called off all his friends with benefits. He never said he had a girlfriend. Ben had to be wrong or mistaken. Maybe he had bad information or something.

I leaned over, my hands resting on my knees for support, as I shook my head before quickly standing back up. "This can't be right," I said, my voice shaking.

"How do you think we know each other?"

"I don't know." I remembered that I had just wondered the same thing.

"Kate's been with him for two years. Why would I lie to you?"

"But he said he broke up with everyone else," I confessed, my voice not sounding like my own.

"When? When did he tell you that? Because I can assure you that they are still together. She just sent me this picture."

I watched as Ben dug out his cell phone and fumbled with it. He shoved a picture in my face. It was Daniel with Kate in his arms, smiles covering both their faces. It looked recent, too recent. Daniel's facial hair in the photo matched exactly the look he currently sported.

Glancing behind me, I noticed Daniel in the distance, his body tense, as I started to fall apart. Tears pooled in my eyes. "I-I," I stuttered. "I have to go."

"I'm really sorry to be the one to tell you, Elizabeth. Maybe we could have dinner soon?"

"Sure. Whatever."

His words hadn't registered. Nothing registered, except the fact that Daniel was a piece-of-shit liar, just like all the others. I dropped the rose he had given me to the ground, and I walked away as quickly as my shaking legs would allow.

heartless

episode 3

Daniel

I watched as Elizabeth all but ran up the street, the opposite direction from where I was waiting for her. *What the hell was going on?*

I started chasing after her, my heart in my fucking throat the whole time as I screamed her name. Ben yelled at me to stop, his footsteps echoing close behind each one of mine.

"Daniel, stop!" he shouted one last time before I felt a pull one my arm. I stopped running and turned to face him, my concern and anger growing.

"What happened? Where is she going?" I growled at Ben.

His grip only tightened, and I gave him one last warning before I completely lost my shit on him.

"What the fuck, Ben? What did you say to her? Let me go before I knock your teeth in."

He tried to contain me, but I flexed both arms before thrashing them back and then down, forcing his grip to loosen. I shoved him, breaking completely free, and he stumbled before trying to regain his balance. He took a shaky step toward me, and I squeezed my right hand into a fist before clocking him square in the jaw. My knuckles throbbed immediately, but I shook it off.

Ben's head flew to the side, and he quickly snapped it back to meet my anger-filled gaze. He charged at me, his face seething, but his over-the-top emotions made him an easy opponent. He stepped toward me with his head down, clearly aiming for my chest, like he was a fucking bull. I stopped him mid-stride with a knee to his ribs. A guttural *oomph* sound escaped as he lowered himself to the pavement, his hand now holding onto his stomach area.

"I'll put you in the fucking ground if you don't knock it off and tell me what the hell is going on—right now."

He glanced up, his eyes wincing in pain. "Why are you cheating on my sister?"

That's what this shit is about? "I'm not cheating on your sister."

He made a girlish grunt sound and I fought back the urge to hit him again. "I just saw you with my own eyes, Daniel. What the hell, man?" He pushed up from the ground and rose to his feet.

"I'm not cheating on your sister," I reiterated. "I ended things with her days ago—right after I met Elizabeth, actually."

"You broke up with my sister for Elizabeth?"

"Ben, I know this won't be easy for you to hear," I paused, knowing that they had a close relationship, "but your sister was never my girlfriend. We were never exclusively dating."

Ben growled as his hand balled into a fist. I dodged the punch and pinched between his neck and shoulder, bringing him down to the ground again.

"Stop fucking trying to hit me. Be pissed, but I never lied to Kate—ever. She knew what it was the whole time."

"Which was what? Some sort of booty call that lasted two years?"

"Yes," I answered honestly. "But she knew that. Damn it, Ben, I'm telling you the truth. She always knew. Right from the start."

"You had to know that she was in love with you." He moved to sit down on top of a knee-high brick wall, his hand palming his jaw.

I followed suit. "I swear to you that I didn't. I would never have guessed it was anything more to her than it was to me."

"She's a girl, Daniel. Girls don't hang around for that long for no reason."

"So I've heard." I shook my head.

"You strung her along. She thought she had a future with you. Hell, she wanted to marry you."

Marry me? What the fuck?

I never alluded to marriage to Kate or any of the other women I'd slept with.

"I never promised her anything of the sort. I am telling you that I was nothing but upfront and honest with her at all times."

"Who fucks a girl for two years without having feelings for her? Who does that?" he asked out loud, his irritation growing.

He truly wasn't hearing a thing I'd said. I sucked in a breath and followed my gut.

"Who tells a girl no guy will ever want her because she's too ambitious?" It was a wild guess, but I knew I was right.

The second Ben had laid eyes on Elizabeth, his face had lit up like a fucking Christmas tree while her face had dropped and then scowled. She hadn't been happy to see Ben, I sensed that immediately.

"What the hell are you talking about?" He looked up at me, his jaw already bruising.

"Elizabeth," I simply said her name—one word, one perfect word.

"Oh Christ, Daniel, that was eight years ago. Apparently, she completely got over that. She seems fine. She's with you, isn't she?" He waved his arm toward where Elizabeth had once stood.

"No, she's clearly not with me, and she's not fine. What did you say to her?"

"I told her that you were dating my sister. I didn't know any different. I warned her to stay away from you." He lowered his head and looked at his feet.

"You what? Motherfucker." I pushed off from the wall and started pacing. "What did you show her on your phone?"

He made a face like he couldn't remember, and I grabbed him by the collar.

"What did you show her?"

"A picture of you and Kate. Kate sent it to me yesterday after I texted and asked how she was. She said that you two were hanging out, having a great day, and then she sent me the photo."

"Yesterday? I haven't seen her in days. Show me."

I had no idea what kind of game Kate was playing, but she was fucking with my life, and I wouldn't have it. I watched as Ben pulled up the text from her, and I saw the picture of Kate and me, smiling. It was the day I'd ended things with her. She'd asked if we could take one last selfie together. I'd warned her that I didn't think it was a good idea, but she'd insisted, and I couldn't tell her no after her meltdown. My guilt was already eating me up inside. I'd figured there was no harm in one last photo with her?

"I should hit you again for not minding your own business."

He raised his hands in surrender. "Sorry. I didn't know. I honestly didn't know. Kate's been lying to us all for years when it came to the two of you." He grabbed his head as if trying to process it all. "But it all makes sense, like why you didn't do any holidays with the family. She always made up excuses for you, but now, I get it."

"Holidays were not a part of the arrangement. That would only confuse things, and I didn't want there to be any confusion. I wanted to avoid this exact scenario," I confessed.

"I really screwed things up for you with Elizabeth, huh? Do you want me to call her and apologize?"

"I'm a grown man. I can handle my own shit with Elizabeth. Why don't you go visit your little sister and make sure she's okay since she's obviously not?"

It wasn't really a request to be honest. My tone demanded that he stay the hell away from Elizabeth and go where he was wanted. Which wasn't anywhere near my girl.

He stood there, shaking his head like a lost dog. "You're right. I should go talk to Kate. Sorry again, man."

I dialed Elizabeth's cell phone three times, but she sent me to voice mail before the third ring. Calling my driver, I had him take me to her apartment before I headed to the airport.

Scanning the list posted next to the front of the door, I found her last name and pressed the small button next to it. The speaker beeped an unholy sound before crackling, and my heart actually fucking leaped into my throat at the idea of her voice coming through the speaker.

Only, it didn't.

The speaker sounded again before clicking, a dial tone replacing the otherwise silent air around me. She had hung up on me before even giving me a chance to speak.

So fucking stubborn.

There had to be something I could do. I stood there, racking my brain, as an older woman exited the building with her tiny dog in tow. She smiled at me, and I grinned back.

"Stuck outside, dear?" she asked.

"My girlfriend is pissed at me and won't let me in. I left my keys upstairs," I half-lied.

She giggled and eyed the single white rose in my hand. I had picked it up from the ground where Elizabeth had dropped it. "Oh, well, you'd better go make it up to her then."

She held the door open, and I bolted up the stairs. Thank God the list outside included the apartment number, otherwise I would have had no idea which direction to head.

I reached the fifth floor and pounded on her door. "Elizabeth! Open the door, and talk to me!"

There were no sounds coming from inside, but I knew she had to be in there. When her next-door neighbor opened his door and glared at me, I apologized for being so loud and promised to keep it down.

Knocking again, I lowered my body against her door and waited for a sign, a sound, anything. Thirty minutes passed before I admitted to myself that she wouldn't see me tonight. Placing the rose in front of her door, I walked away, accepting my current defeat.

Elizabeth

Daniel called my cell phone three times before I finally turned it off, my heart unable to deal with whatever he needed to say to me tonight. I hopped in the shower and allowed my tears to fall.

How could I have been so stupid as to think someone like Daniel would ever be a one-woman kind of guy?

He'd told me that he ended things with those other women, and I'd simply believed him, no questions asked.

Why?

I knew the answer, but it made me feel stupid inside. I wanted to be special. When we'd talked the night we met about girls wanting to be different to a guy, that was exactly what Daniel had convinced me I was, and I'd bought into it completely. It hurt. I hurt. Before Daniel, I'd shut myself off from feeling vulnerable for so long that this seemed like it might crush me from the weight.

I sucked in a raspy breath and settled into bed before reaching for my iPod and noise-canceling headphones. Music always soothed me, and tonight, I needed it more than I ever had before.

When I woke up the next morning, I was reluctant to switch on my cell. For a minute, I wondered if I could exist an entire day without it. Deciding that probably wasn't the best idea, I turned it on and watched as it powered up. A lengthy text message from Daniel appeared, telling me that Ben had it all wrong. Daniel wanted to explain things to me, and he begged me not to jump to conclusions.

Too late.

I had already jumped headfirst into that picture Ben had shown me and into the words he had said.

When I exited my apartment door, I almost stepped on the white rose lying across my blue doormat. *He had been here? When?*

Apparently, my headphones had helped drown out more than just my feelings.

Barbara's long legs walked into my office, and then she plopped down on my couch with a thud.

"What's the matter?" I asked, hoping for any conversation other than the kind that revolved around Daniel.

"I had a shitty date last night. Please tell me all about how fabulous yours was with Mr. Perfect, so I can be insanely jealous."

Avoiding all things Daniel didn't last long. I forced a smile. "Mr. Perfect? More like Mr. I'm Still Dating Other Women."

Her eyes widened as she leaned forward. "Excuse me? He's what?"

"We had the most amazing dinner. The conversation, the food—it was…" I struggled to find the right word without being cliché. "Perfect. It was perfect."

"So, what happened?"

"We walked outside and ran into Ben."

Her jaw dropped. "Ben, Ben? Like, your ex Ben?"

"Yeah."

"Oh my God. Is that the first time you've seen him since college?"

Sucking in a quick breath, I moved my hand toward my upset stomach. "Yeah. Can you believe that? Anyway, he pulled me aside—"

"Ben pulled you aside?" she interrupted, clearly wanting to get all the facts straight.

I nodded. "So, he pulled me aside and asked me what I was doing there with Daniel."

"What the fuck business is it of his? Wait—he knows Daniel? How does he know Daniel?" Her brows pulled together with her sudden confusion.

"If you'd let me finish, then you could stop giving yourself wrinkles."

Her expression immediately softened as she rubbed a finger across the bridge of her nose like she could erase any creases that wanted to form there. "Finish."

"So, Ben pulled me aside and asked me what I was doing there with Daniel. I told him it was none of his business, but he told me that Daniel was his business. I asked him why that was, and he said because Daniel was dating his sister!"

"No." Her head started shaking with her disbelief. "Nope. I don't believe it."

"Ben showed me a picture of them together."

"So what? Were they fucking in said picture?"

I choked out a breath. "No."

"Were they kissing?" she continued, her tone completely unconvinced.

"No."

"What were they doing then?"

"Just sitting there with their faces squished together. They looked cozy, friendly. Whatever. They looked like more than friends," I all but shouted.

Barbara rose to her feet. "Have you talked to him? How did things end?"

"I left."

"With or without Daniel?"

"Without."

"And you haven't talked to him since, have you?"

I shook my head. "I feel like an idiot. I was hurting. I believed Daniel when he said he called off his arrangements. I fell for his charm and his stupid hot face."

"Elizabeth, you don't need to feel stupid unless you don't give him a chance to explain his side of things. I understand that this is all new to you, but you can't run away from him like you're a child. He isn't Ben, and you're not the same girl you were when Ben cheated on you. You're a grown woman, so act like it."

"Jeez, Barbara, easy on the tough love. I'm a little rusty."

"Sorry. I just really like Daniel. I, for one, don't think he's lying to you. I know a bullshitter when I meet one. While I think he could bullshit with the best of them, I don't think he does when it comes to you. But you'll never know if you don't talk to him like grown-ups do. Be a grown-up."

"Being a grown-up is dumb," I whined.

"Running away is dumber."

Elizabeth

Barbara's admonishment of me made me question my every action from last night. She was right though. I wasn't the same girl who had once dated Ben. I had grown, and I shouldn't even think about handling Daniel the same way I would have handled this sort of situation eight years ago. I needed to suck it up and give him a chance to explain.

If it turned out that he was nothing more than a lying sack of shit, then I could hang his nuts from my rearview mirror. But I wouldn't do anything rash before knowing the facts.

Whatever the truth was needed to wait because of my busy schedule for the day, but it really couldn't wait too long because of my pounding heart. I needed to get my head out of this crap and focus on my job, but dealing with Daniel would be the only way for me to do that. He had twisted me up since the day I met him, and I needed some clarity.

My legs shook under my desk as I reached for my phone, nervousness and anxiety screaming through me all at once. It would be one thing if Daniel were the one calling, but it was me calling him, and that very fact freaked me out. I scrolled through my contacts until I reached his name. Pressing Send, I held my breath and pressed my lips together as I waited for the call to connect.

"Elizabeth." My name sounded so beautiful coming from his lips. "I'm so glad you called. Can you give me a second?"

"Sure," I answered, my throat feeling instantly parched.

Daniel yelled in the background for someone to give him ten minutes, and I heard the distinct sound of a door shutting before he was back.

"You there?"

"I'm here," I breathed out, wishing I had some water.

"So, about last night—" he started to explain before I cut him off.

"Me first. I'm sorry I ran away without even giving you the chance to talk to me about it. I know that was immature of me, but I was so upset, and I just honestly figured that you'd lied to me."

His breath heaved through the phone as I waited for him to speak, yell, chastise me, or something.

"Listen to me, Elizabeth. I'm not going to pretend to be happy about the way things went down last night, but I realize that we both have our own issues when it comes to relationships."

"You can say that again," I said, mostly speaking for myself.

"I'm not done," he snapped.

I immediately quieted.

"This is all new to me, too. Having a girlfriend isn't something I've done in a long time. It's not something I've ever wanted to do lately, but I want to—with you. You have to trust me though. I know that trust is earned, but *I'm not a liar*," he emphasized, making his point crystal clear. "I've never lied to you, and I never will. You have to believe that in order for this to work."

"You're right. You're so right, and I'm sorry. I just saw that picture of you and Kate, and I couldn't breathe. The way I feel about you frightens me."

"How do you feel about me?" he questioned, his tone lightening up.

"I like you." I paused. "A lot."

"I like you a lot, too," he mimicked.

"I'm not done," I pretend snapped. "Thinking that you were still dating someone or that you lied to me about calling off your other women was so hurtful. We've just started dating, but I feel things for you that I've never felt before. You have the power to wreck me, Daniel, completely fucking wreck me, and that absolutely terrifies me."

"Welcome to the club."

"Huh?" I questioned.

"You think you're the only one risking getting hurt here?"

"I don't know. I have no idea if you have the same feelings that I do."

"I'm the one who's been pursuing you. I'm the one chasing you down and making new rules because I can't stand the thought of being without you."

"I'm making new rules, too." I added. Not too long ago, I'd sworn that I'd never date anyone, let alone him.

"Then, stop acting like you're alone in this. We're in this together." His tone was more than reassuring.

As I listened to him, my heart swelled, the shriveling organ matter it had become last night slowly refilling again.

"Is there anything else?" he asked.

"What do you mean, anything else?"

"Do you have any other concerns?"

"Aside from you annihilating my very being?" I tried to tease, but I wasn't kidding.

"Yes, Elizabeth, aside from that." He huffed out a laugh.

I chewed on a pen cap, wondering if I should say the first thing that popped into my head.

"What are you afraid of? Tell me, so I can prove you wrong."

"I'm scared of you, of losing myself in you and forgetting who I am," I admitted, feeling weaker than I'd ever felt. It was one thing to be a strong businesswoman in an industry filled with men, but it was something entirely different when my heart was on the line, and emotions were involved.

"I'll never let that happen, and you won't either."

"How do you know?"

"Because you're too strong of a person to lose everything you've worked for, and I'll never let you. I won't allow you to fall or lose focus. I want you to be great. I want you to be successful."

His words made me feel like I was floating on air. I swore, if I looked down, I'd see my desk and lamps below me and the ceiling at my fingertips.

"Is this how real relationships are supposed to work?"

"I think so. What are your thoughts so far?"

"Healthy communication, reassurance, building each other up instead of tearing each other down?" I paused. "I like it."

"I love it. I'll see you tonight."

"What?"

"You think I'm staying up here after our first fight? How will we have make-up sex if I'm five hundred miles away?"

"Oh my gosh. You really are presumptuous. Good-bye, Daniel." I laughed before ending the call.

I was excited. Daniel hadn't lied to me, he wasn't dating anyone else, and I was getting laid tonight. *Maybe.* I only hoped Barbara wasn't right about my hoo-ha being broken or out of business or any other strange thing she'd suggested was wrong with it because apparently I'd need it later. *Was I really ready to take this step with him?* I'd know for sure once I saw him later.

Daniel

Thank God Elizabeth had called me. I would have gone half mad if I had to go the whole day without talking to her. Getting through the night had been hell enough.

"James, get back in here!" I yelled, knowing he was most likely waiting right outside my door.

He burst back into my office. "What happened? I'm dying here."

"You're such a chick. Anyone ever tell you that?"

"Yeah." He looked straight at me before getting comfortable on my recliner. "You—all the time. So what? Tell me what happened."

"She apologized, and we're good," I said with a smile.

"That's it?"

I shrugged, not knowing what the fuck else he wanted. "What else is there? She said she was sorry for running away, I accepted, and we'll fuck later. The end. Happy?"

"You're flying down there again? Why don't you just move?" He pushed back in the chair and eyeballed me.

"Funny."

"Twenty bucks says you'll move for this girl before the end of the year."

"Fifty bucks says I'll fire you before that."

He laughed. "I'm just saying, we've always talked about having an office down there."

"No one cares about what you're saying," I joked. "Now, tell me you looked over that proposal."

James straightened the recliner as he leaned forward, putting his elbows on his knees. "You were right. That one design issue will eventually backfire, causing frivolous lawsuits left and right. They'll lose everything if they don't address it before they release. What's the status on their end?"

"They think I'm wrong."

James slapped his leg. "So, we're out then." He knew damn well I'd never knowingly go through with a flawed investment. "Good luck, boys."

"We're out," I agreed.

"Can I call them? Oh, please let me be the one to tell them they need to find new investors. I love that part." He was practically foaming at the mouth.

"You're a sick fuck, you know that? You're the only guy I know who gets off on crushing people's dreams."

"That is not true." He waved a finger at me. "I only get off on it when they deserve it. When they're too arrogant to see reality, it gives me great pleasure to bring down the hammer."

I smiled and nodded my head in agreement. Silently, I was thankful that James liked dealing with this aspect of the business. It made my life easier to be the decision-maker but not the one who delivered the news, especially when it wasn't what people wanted to hear.

"What are you gonna do about Kate?"

His question surprised me, and I shot him a look.

"What do you mean?"

"Are you just going to let her continue to freak out? Or are you going to talk to her?"

"Last night I strongly suggested to Ben that he pay his little sister a visit. My concerns lie with Elizabeth, not with Kate."

"So whipped."

"Don't even care."

"This is great. Please tell me she has a hot friend for me." He wagged his eyebrows, and I wanted to throw something at him again.

My mind instantly saw Barbara's face. I knew how much he'd fucking love her and vice versa, but I wasn't sure if even mentioning that would be a good idea while Elizabeth and I were still sorting ourselves out.

"She's too busy with work. She doesn't socialize much," I half-lied.

She never talked about her girlfriends, but I never found it strange. If it wasn't for James, I'd never talk or hang out with anyone either.

"You're lying, but that's fine. I'm just going to come down with you next time, and I'll see for myself," he informed me with a stupid smirk.

"Next time is in a few hours, and you're not invited."

"Not tonight. Next time, next time."

"Don't you have work to do? People's hearts to shatter? Get to it."

He saluted me and gave me a smug-ass grin before walking out.

Elizabeth

I offered to pick Daniel up from the Santa Monica airport, and we drove to my house in awkward anticipation of what the night held. At least I felt awkward. He seemed perfectly fine. Then again, he'd had sex far more recently than I had.

"You look beautiful," he said before placing his hand on my thigh.

I felt my cheeks warm as I blushed with his compliment.

"Thank you." I briefly glanced over at him before paying attention to the traffic-laden streets.

"Is it always this busy here?" His face was tilted to the right as he looked out at the streets.

"For the most part. Everyone seems to come here all day, and then they never leave at night."

"What do you mean?"

"Well, there is so much to do here. People spend the day at the beach, and then they shop all night or go to dinner. We have tons of restaurants and bars. It's the ideal tourist spot. Remind me to take you to one of my favorite places sometime, okay? It's completely underrated."

"Let's go now," his voice purred.

My heart raced. I knew if we delayed the inevitable any longer, I'd fall apart with the expectation of what was to come.

"It's not open now," I half-lied. It most likely wasn't open right now even though I knew I could get us in.

"Fine. Take me home already." He smirked.

"I'm trying," I said, braking as another streetlight turned red.

Two right turns later, and we pulled into the underground parking lot of my building. Shutting off the engine, I exited the car and made my way to the passenger side, a full dozen white roses tied with a string from Daniel in hand.

He grabbed me and I almost dropped the few things in my arms. "I hate that we fought."

"Me, too." I looked into his hazel eyes and melted.

"But I like that we get to make up." He pressed his lips to mine, his hand reaching back to grip my ass. "I can't wait to make you mine."

I shivered as he followed me through the parking garage and toward the elevator against the well-lit corner of the building. He wasted no time once the doors had closed. His body shoved against mine, his hand making sure to cradle the back of my head so that it wouldn't slam into the hardness of the elevator wall. Tongues frantically searched for one another as his hands roamed over my body in places where I wouldn't have dared let him touch me a mere few days ago.

He pulled away only slightly, looking me in the eyes before saying, "You're so fucking beautiful, Elizabeth, and smart and feisty and a pain in my ass. You have no idea what you do to me."

I reached across the front of his suit pants and cupped his growing dick. "I have some sort of idea," I said as my cheeks warmed with his compliments and my excitement.

His lips grazed against my neck, sucking and licking, causing my eyes to squeeze shut with pleasure. The elevator dinged, and I reached for his hand, my chest heaving with each breath I took.

"This way," I said, pulling him down the hallway toward my door.

"It's too far," he complained before stopping and yanking my body against his.

One hand gripped my lower back, pinning me against his hard-on, while the other tangled in my hair and pulled.

I moaned against his lips, into his mouth, and on his tongue.

I reached for his cheeks, gripping the rough exterior between my palms, in order to keep his face still and his mouth on mine. He laughed into me, and I smiled.

"We're almost there," I reassured him as I continued to step backward.

"We'll have to do it here. Get naked," he said, pointing at the carpeted flooring.

I hurried toward my door, only a few feet away.

"I bet you say that to all the girls. Can we go inside now?" I asked before unlocking the door.

He extended one arm to hold it open and waved me inside before following right behind. I placed the keys and roses on the kitchen counter, as Daniel moved to pin my body against it.

"I don't have any more girls, remember? Just want to be clear on that subject."

"I remember. That's why I let you come over," I said playfully.

"You were going to let me come over anyway."

"Yeah, but I wouldn't have let you touch me."

His lips pressed against my neck as his tongue paved a way lower. "This dress is so fucking sexy." He lowered the sleeve with his fingertips before his mouth followed. "I can't wait to see it on the floor."

"What good will it be on the floor?" I asked with a coy smile.

"It will be great 'cause then you'll be naked. Guys like naked."

"So predictable," I teased, moving my body away from him and heading toward my bedroom.

I watched his eyes as they glanced toward my bedroom window.

"Shit, what a view."

My eyes followed, catching sight of the sun setting and the orange glow it cast across the water. "I love living here."

"I can see why. Hell, Elizabeth, I'd work from home all the time."

"That's exactly why I have to force myself to go to the office every day. I'd never get any work done. Do you know how hard it is to see that outside your window and stay indoors? Fuck that."

He growled at my words, his body against mine in a flash. "Yeah, fuck that." His mouth found my neck again as he sucked and pushed me toward the bed, his hand firmly on my lower back.

My legs touched the edge of the mattress before Daniel lifted me by my ass and tossed me on top. He all but crawled over me, his movements slow and deliberate, and then he lowered himself on top of me.

"We have too many clothes on," he said as he pushed off me. Resting back on his knees, he started to remove his tie.

"Stop. Let me," I demanded as I pushed myself up to face him.

I wanted to undress him. This sexual act had been such a long time coming for me that I wanted to revel in being a woman doing it, as opposed to a naive girl. He immediately dropped his arms to his sides as I went to work. My hands reached for his crisp black shirt and started unbuttoning the buttons, one by one. Each release was followed by a peek of tanned skin that I kissed with my mouth and licked with my tongue. Daniel moaned, his fingers tangling in my hair more with each touch of my lips on his bare skin. I reached the last button, and my mouth was incredibly close to the waist of his pants.

"You might be the death of me, woman," he said.

I glanced up to meet his gaze. "I just found you. Don't die yet."

I moved to free the shirt from his body, and he wiggled his arms to get out of it, like he couldn't shed his second skin quickly enough. My eyes roamed every exposed inch of his bare chest and arms. My want for him grew as my gaze lingered on his defined abs and the muscles in his shoulders.

"See something you like?" he mimicked his words from the first night we'd met.

I laughed. "Definitely, and it's not the floor this time."

I reached for the back of his neck and pulled him down on top of me. Our mouths opened and closed, our tongues dancing with one another.

"This dress—I need it off. Now."

"So bossy."

"So don't care. Stand up."

He pushed away from me once more and stood beside the bed. His hand reached for mine, and he pulled me to my feet and spun me around, my back facing him. He moved my hair to the side before kissing my neck. With each tormenting pull of the zipper, he kissed my back until his lips reached right above my ass. With full clarity, I knew what I had just done to him. The zipper going no further, he reached for my shoulders once more before turning me back around to face him. The material easily fell off my body without any effort, and I stepped out of it, my breasts uncovered.

"No bra, Elizabeth? You don't wear a bra to work?" His voice took on a timbre that I could only interpret as desire.

"The dress has one built in, so no." I stood there, feeling completely exposed, in nothing but a black lacy thong.

Daniel lowered his mouth to my left breast before taking it in. His tongue licked around my nipple as he bit at it lightly with his teeth. My fingers tangled in his dark hair as I tossed my head back and sucked in quick breaths. He moved to my right one and nibbled at it first before squeezing and licking it while my thighs quivered with desire.

Feeling underdressed and bare, I reached for the belt on his pants and undid it before threading the button through the hole and lowering the zipper. His suit pants dropped, and he stepped out of them, our clothes a pool of fabric on my floor. My eyes landed squarely on the package in his boxer briefs, the bulge begging to be unleashed.

Daniel expertly moved our bodies back onto the bed, each of our most private parts covered by thin cloth. When his nearly naked body touched mine, I almost screamed out with pleasure. His skin on my skin sent feelings racing through me that I could only describe as primal lust. The feeling of him pressed against me was overwhelming, and I wanted more.

"Your skin is so soft," he breathed into my ear. "Wait right here. I'll be right back."

He hopped off the bed before I could protest, and he returned carrying one of the roses he must have grabbed from the kitchen. I smiled at the view of my naked man holding nothing but a single rose.

"See something you like?" he asked with a wink.

"Ugh, you and that line," I answered, rolling my eyes.

He lowered his body next to mine and kissed my stomach before replacing his soft lips with the velvet feel of rose petals. Daniel moved the rose down to the tops of my toes before forcing it to travel up the length of my leg in painfully slow motion. My eyes closed at the sheer eroticism of it all.

Who knew rose petals felt this way on your naked skin?

I moaned out loud, and Daniel's lips kissed my thigh as goosebumps appeared across my skin..

"I just wanted to take my time here. I hope you don't mind." He laughed. "Not that you have any say in the matter."

My breath hitched, and I was unable to respond, unsure of what I would say anyway. Reaching for his head, I weaved my fingers in his dark hair and massaged the top of his head as he continued to sweetly torment me with the rose and his mouth.

The petals reached my stomach, and I sucked in a quick breath as he swirled it around my belly button in a gentle movement. His lips followed the rose, kissing each place the rose petals touched, until I could no longer differentiate between the softness of his mouth and the softness of the petals. With my eyes closed, I was in my own blissful world.

Daniel pulled the rose away, and I opened my eyes in time to see him pluck the petals from the perfect flower.

"What are you doing?"

"I'm going to kiss you where each petal lands."

I watched as he dropped a fistful of white petals down the length of my naked body. Rose petals rained across parts of my body that had never touched a rose before. My breathing became shallow, so none of the petals would fall from where they'd landed, as my anticipation continued to build.

Daniel's head started at my neck where two petals had settled. He gently brushed them aside and licked where they'd once lain. I fought back the urge to arch my back and grab him.

Daniel said, "Don't make the petals fall, Elizabeth, or I'll have to start all over."

Smiling, his lips lowered to my décolletage. He kissed and licked in small circles over my skin before moving to where the next petal lay. Daniel's wet tongue explored my breasts as euphoria coursed through me with each touch. Hot air breezed across my stomach as he blew at the pieces of white. Some simply moved to another area of my body while others fell to my sides.

"Daniel." My voice came out in a whisper.

He glanced up at me. "Yes?"

"You're torturing me," I admitted breathlessly.

He smiled. "I know." His head dipped back down, and he followed the few remaining rose petals. "This is the sweetest one." He moved the petal on top of my lace panties aside and kissed the fabric.

Heat from his mouth seared through the lace and pierced my skin as my need for him soared. I was fairly certain I might die if he didn't take this further.

"I need to be inside you, Elizabeth."

Thank God. "I want you so much," I reassured him, not that he needed it. "Please."

His fingers found the top of my panties and pulled at them, moving them down my thighs, and I wiggled to help get them completely off.

He looked down at me and sucked in a quick breath. "So fucking beautiful. God, you really are."

His hands were all over me, his mouth sucking and licking, and I squeezed my eyes closed with the pure pleasure he elicited from me.

I found the waistband of his boxer briefs and attempted the same maneuver, but I couldn't reach nearly as far. His hand joined mine and helped to pull them off. The tip of his dick pushed against me for a second, and I gasped. I wanted this man. I wanted all of him—now.

"Tell me you brought a condom." I hoped I wasn't ruining the moment.

"A condom? Hell, babe, I brought the whole box." He moved toward the edge of the bed and reached for his pants before fishing a strip of them out of his pocket.

I heard the long-forgotten sound of foil tearing open, and Daniel sat facing me, his dick at full attention as he rolled it on. I stared at it like I was seeing one for the first time. With my head lying against the pillow, he lowered his body over mine, his shoulders bearing the brunt of his muscular frame. His muscles flexed as his mouth found mine and my eyes closed. His tongue grazed over my bottom lip before entering. The tip of his dick found my most sensitive area again, and my hips bucked up and rolled, silently pleading with him to enter.

My eyes opened, and I found Daniel watching me, staring at me. His eyes locked on mine, like he was memorizing everything about this moment. Our connection seemed so deep, so fierce, and I never wanted it to end. He pushed slowly into me, with care, and my mouth opened with the slight ache. It had been so long for me, but the pleasure far outweighed any discomfort.

"Are you okay?" he asked before moving all the way in.

My fingers dug into his back, pulling him to me. "Yes," I exhaled. "I want you."

He breathed out a quick huff of air before pushing himself deep inside me, and I moaned with the feeling of him filling me.

"Elizabeth," he growled before moving in and out.

I rocked my hips in time with his. "You feel so good," I whispered. "So fucking good."

I had no idea what I'd been missing all these years that I'd banned men, but I wagered that most of my experiences wouldn't have been anything like this. This was more than just a physical act. It was sensual, filled with emotions, and that always made sex better.

"You feel amazing." He continued to move before running his fingers down my cheek. "I love being inside you. You're perfect."

I glanced away with his compliment before saying, "Stop."

"What?" His body immediately stilled.

"I want on top." I tried to push his shoulders over so that his body would move.

His devilish grin appeared. "Your wish is my command." He rolled over, seamlessly taking my body with his, never breaking our connection.

Lowering myself completely on top of him, my mouth opened again as pleasure coursed through me. His hands reached for my sides, and they directed my pace. I rolled my hips, my body moving forward and back on him, and I felt him growing even larger inside me.

"Jesus, babe, I'm gonna come," he warned.

I smiled, knowing that I was the one bringing him such pleasure. My movements quickened as his fingertips dug into my sides, my body moving on him, against him, with him.

"Oh, Daniel," I said as I rode him even harder. "Oh God." My body quaked as the orgasm soared through me, forcing even my toes to curl.

Daniel bucked into me, using his hands to move me up and down as he jerked slightly, and his body tightened. His eyes squeezed tight, and I watched as his jaw clenched and unclenched with his orgasm. He reopened his eyes, and a smile formed across his lips.

"You're incredible." He pushed up to kiss me before moving me off his lap. He stood up from the bed, his condom-covered dick still at full attention. "Bathroom?" he asked.

I pointed to the door, my breathing still erratic. I fell onto the bed, grabbed the sheet, and pulled it against my chest as my heart raced.

When he reappeared, he was smiling.

"What are you so happy about?" I asked.

His smile grew deeper. "Like you need to ask." He winked before sliding into bed next to me and planting a kiss on my cheek. "We should definitely fight more often."

I laughed. "No, we shouldn't, but we should definitely do *that* more often."

"Just give me thirty minutes to recover, and I'm all yours." He pulled my naked body against his and held me tight.

"Thirty minutes? You're an old man."

He huffed, "Yeah? I'll show you *old man*"—his fingers playfully scratched against my side—"in thirty minutes."

Elizabeth

Daniel left before my alarm blared, and I awoke to a single white rose sitting on my nightstand. How he'd had the time to get a rose before he left town, I had absolutely no idea, but I appreciated the sentiment. It was the first time since meeting him that I truly hated the fact that he lived so far away.

I ached for him, and the very idea that I wouldn't get to see him when I got home from work made me sad. The logical part of my brain tried in vain to silence my heart, reminding it that I'd lived just fine for years without Daniel Alexander by my side. But my heart refused to listen to logic. It was too ecstatic at being so excited by a man.

Stupid heart—oh, how I love you.

I strode onto the studio lot, my feet reacting as if they were dancing on clouds with each step.

"Oh my gosh." Barbara rose to greet me.

Without stopping, I walked straight into my office, and she followed before shutting the door behind her.

"You totally got laid last night. You have sex face!"

Laughing, I turned around to face her. "What the hell is sex face? And how do you always know these things?" I rushed to my desk and dropped into my chair.

"You already know that my vagina has superpowers." She winked before slamming her hands down on my desk and sitting across from me. "I want to know every dirty, disgusting detail."

"Uh…no," I tried to argue, not wanting to fill anyone in on the details of my night with Daniel.

Barbara knowing we'd had sex should be more than enough information.

She crossed her arms and pouted. "Fine. But, honestly, you look really happy and relaxed. I should have gotten you laid years ago."

"And we say you're the romantic one." I smiled, sorting through the scripts and notes on my desk.

"By the way, Ben keeps calling you. I keep"—she made air quotes with her fingers—"*forgetting* to tell you."

"Ben? Why? What does he want?"

The idea of Ben calling me made me irritated. Seeing him hadn't truly fazed me like I thought it might, and I wanted to forget the whole thing had ever happened, especially the part that included his little sister screwing Daniel.

"I think seeing you messed him up. He sounds desperate every time he calls. His voice is shaky and off."

"If I'm available the next time, just put him through."

"Also…" she dragged out the word.

"Spit it out. What the heck is wrong with you this morning?" I stopped shuffling through my papers to eyeball her.

"Mr. Kline is on a rampage. He's in a foul mood, already stomping around over here and slamming doors shut over there."

"Great. I'm meeting with him in twenty."

"I know. Just giving you a heads-up. Happy day-after-sex day!" She pushed back from the chair she was in and strode out of my office.

I sucked in a quick breath, determined not to let anything affect my newly blissful state of mind.

"I need a shower." I started stripping off the few pieces of workout clothing I wore. I kicked off my shoes and socks on the living room floor before peeling off my tank top and dropping it as well.

I pretended not to notice Daniel following behind me. I slipped out of my shorts and deposited them in the hallway. Daniel still pursued me, picking up each item as I dropped it. My sports bra landed on my bedroom floor, and I heard him groan with pleasure. My underwear almost made it into the bathroom but not quite. His hands were all over me in that moment, before his mouth joined in.

I shoved him away. "Let me take a shower before you taste me all over, please. I'm disgusting."

He smiled and sucked in his bottom lip. "I'm coming in. This whole shower thing is not happening without me."

"If you insist."

Being completely naked in a brightly lit shower with a man was one of the most personal things you could do, in my opinion, aside from holding his penis in your mouth. But right now, I was so blinded by my desire for him that I didn't care if I looked fluffy in this lighting or if my body wasn't quite perfect. The lust pumping through my veins and the fully erect penis I was staring at helped any insecurities I might have had fade away in that instant. I wanted him, and I didn't care about anything else.

"See something you like?" He winked, and I stopped myself from smacking his arm.

"Not sure. Looks sort of..." I paused, my intention to torment him and mess with his head clearly working by the look on his face.

"Looks sort of what?" he growled before looking down and waving a hand. "Get in the shower. I'll show you what it looks like."

It looked big, intimidating, but it was far more fun to tease Daniel Alexander than it was to stroke his...ego.

The water hit my face, and I closed my eyes, reveling in the feel of it against my skin. Daniel's hands wrapped around my midsection, his fingers splayed across my stomach, as he worked to turn me around. His mouth briefly met mine with fervor before moving down to my exposed breasts. He nipped and sucked my nipple into his mouth, and my knees trembled. As he visited each breast, giving them both proper attention, I moaned before he started kissing down the middle of my stomach.

When he dropped to his knees, my fingers fisted his hair, saying everything my lips currently couldn't. I didn't want him to stop. His tongue pressed against my sex before licking two times, and a sound escaped my lips that I would swear couldn't have come from me. Tossing my head back, I pulled his face harder against my body. He continued to lap me up, his tongue exploring every inch of my most sensitive area, as pure pleasure ripped through my body with each stroke of his tongue.

"Elizabeth? Elizabeth, have you even heard a word I've said during the last ten minutes? Elizabeth!"

What the fuck?

Shaking my head, I refocused my eyes, Daniel's naked image disappearing as Mr. Kline's private boardroom came into view. His beady brown eyes bore into me from behind his wire-rimmed glasses.

Shit. Shit. Shit.

"Mr. Kline, I'm so sorry." I glanced around the room filled with men, feeling like an absolute idiot.

They all stared at me, silently judging and feeling thankful that it wasn't happening to them.

"What is going on with you lately?" Mr. Kline growled and slammed a hand on the table, making his pen roll onto the floor. "Tell me what was so great in your fucking head that you didn't hear a word I've said."

Seriously? "I'm sorry. I must have drifted off to this book I started reading this morning. It's extremely addictive, and I can't stop thinking about what might happen next with the main characters," I lied through my teeth, hoping like hell he'd buy what I was desperately trying to sell him.

"Adaptation worthy?" He suddenly seemed less angry.

"I hope so. I'll know for sure once I've read the whole story."

"I want a presentation on why it is, or isn't, worthy of pursuing once you finish reading it," he demanded.

"Of course," I agreed before realizing that I needed to find a brilliant book to read—pronto.

The rest of the meeting went on without any more daydreams on my end. I needed to get it together. This very thing was exactly why I'd stayed away from men in the first place. Daniel could not make it impossible for me to function during the days, or this wasn't going to work, not one bit.

Daniel

It absolutely sucked leaving Elizabeth's place this morning, and I'd had to force myself to go. Everything in my body had wanted to stay by her side, hold her until she woke up, and then send her to work with my scent all over her. I was like a fucking dog in heat, wanting to mark his territory.

With my phone, I'd snapped a picture of her sleeping, her blonde hair splayed across the pillow and down her back while she looked so peaceful. It was the only picture I had of her, and right now, I was so fucking thankful that I had been such a psycho and taken it. Looking at her beautiful face brought me utter joy.

I had officially turned into a pussy.

Two knocks on the door, and James walked into my office, a bottle of water tucked under his arm.

I placed my cell phone down. *Perfect timing.*

"How was last night, buddy?"

He made himself at home on my couch, and I made a mental note to purchase a Nerf gun for future meetings like this.

"How many times do I have to tell you to go lie down on your own couch? This isn't your bedroom." I pretended to be annoyed as I imagined pummeling him with a dozen rubber darts at once.

"You've been saying that for years."

"You're a good listener."

"Ha-ha. So, tell me about last night," he said again.

I glared at my best friend, my mouth shut tight, until he swung his feet from my furniture and moved to a normal sitting position.

"Better?"

"Much." I smirked.

"Are you going to tell me? Or am I flying down there and asking her myself?"

I bristled. "Don't fucking talk like that. You know I'd beat your ass. You'll meet her when I allow it."

"Anyone ever tell you that you're a control freak?"

"Anyone ever tell you that you're a pain in the ass?"

He shook his head and opened the cap on a bottle of water before taking a swig. "Mostly you. Every day. Good thing my confidence can handle it."

"Yeah, you clearly have a confidence issue." I gave him a little head nod before huffing out a laugh. "Last night was great."

"When isn't sex great?"

"When it sucks," I said, my tone serious.

His hands flew up in defense of his stupid words. "Okay, okay. I meant, when isn't sex great when you actually like the chick?"

"Stop calling her a chick."

"Buddy, you are so far gone with this one. Should we go shopping for china patterns later? Should I tell Serena to clear your schedule for the rest of the day?"

Damn it. Where is that Nerf gun when I need it?

"Why don't you ever have anything else to do?"

He leaned back and placed his feet on top of my coffee table. "Harassing you is more fun."

"Get your feet off my table. Were you raised in a barn? I know for a fact that you fucking weren't. Don't make me call your mother."

He promptly moved his feet. "You wouldn't dare."

I wiggled my eyebrows. "I so would."

"You play hardball, man. Now, seriously, tell me more about what happened. Everything good with you and your future wife?"

"Shut up, dickhole."

"You know I'm just giving you shit," he stared at me. "Now tell me what happened dammit."

I sighed, half temped to ask him if he needed a tampon to go with his whining, but I digressed.

"It was fucking great. She's great. I've never met anyone more in sync with me. I don't know. We just get each other, you know?" I looked at him before shaking my head. "Of course you don't know. Why the hell am I telling you any of this?"

"Because I'm your best friend. But sometimes, Daniel, your words hurt." He threw his hand over his heart in mock pain.

"Oh my God, get out of here, and go do something that makes me money."

"Fine." He stood up. "But only 'cause you asked so nice."

Once I heard the door shut, I sorted my emails, searching for ones that needed immediate attention, as my thoughts filled with Elizabeth. Her naked body entered my mind, and my dick started to harden. Just a single thought of her had us both pining for more. I needed to fly her up here. I wanted her here, in my space, where I could take her in every corner of my office, home, and plane.

Elizabeth Lyons had turned me into a fucking sex fanatic.

Reaching for the phone, I dialed her office line.

"Elizabeth Lyons's office. This is Barbara."

"Whatcha wearing?" I teased, not meaning the question at all.

Thankfully, Barbara knew that.

"Granny panties, jean overalls, and a long-sleeved shirt." She laughed into the phone.

"Sounds hot. Send me a pic." I tried to keep a straight face, not that she could see it.

"Elizabeth's in a meeting. I'll have her call you as soon as she gets out, if she has a chance."

"Sounds good. Tell her I miss her."

Barbara cooed, "That's so sweet. I'll tell her. Bye."

Elizabeth

After the meeting ended, I started to think that maybe I wasn't the type of person who could balance both a relationship and a successful career. Because if this was how adult Elizabeth behaved, it wasn't going to work.

What happened today could never happen again. Who daydreamed about shower sex in the middle of a presentation with the head of the studio? Then again, who wouldn't daydream about shower sex with Daniel Alexander?

No.

Damn it.

This was the exact problem and issue I'd always wanted to avoid in my life. I needed to refocus.

As I neared Barbara's desk, her face lit up. "Daniel called. He wanted you to know he misses you."

My heart fluttered with her words, causing my body to declare war on itself. It was officially on—heart versus brain.

I tried to keep a straight face, acting like I wasn't affected. "Anyone else?"

"Ben and someone named Kate. She left her number. She sounded odd."

My breath stammered. "Kate?"

"Yeah, who is she?"

"Ben's sister," I said, wondering why in the world Kate was calling me at my place of employment.

"The one Daniel—" Barbara practically shouted.

I cut her off, holding one hand in the air, "Don't say it, but yes."

"Well, that's weird, right?"

"Very." I turned into my office.

I placed my notes on my desk and stared at the call log online. *Why the hell had Kate called me? And why wouldn't Ben stop?*

Pulling my cell phone out of my purse, I noticed a text from Daniel.

It's ridiculous how much I miss you.

I stared at it for a full minute before deciding not to respond. For whatever reason, I held Daniel at fault for my daydreaming this morning, and I was pissed at him for it. I wanted someone to blame, and I refused to blame myself.

After putting away my cell, I dialed Ben's number from my office phone and massaged my temples as it rang.

"Elizabeth, babe!" he shouted into the phone.

"Dear God, I'm not your babe. What do you need, Ben?"

"Aw, don't be like that. I told you the other night that I thought we should grab dinner. I'd like to see you, for old times' sake. Please. I want to talk to you about some things." His voice took on a tone that I hadn't heard in years. It was the same way he used to talk to me when we'd dated in college and he'd wanted to get his way on something. He sounded like a child, and I wondered how I'd ever found that stupid tone endearing.

"What things exactly?" I pressed, unsure of where he was headed.

"Come on, Elizabeth. Just have dinner with me."

"I really can't. I don't have time. I'm under a production deadline, and I'm going to be at the office late for the next few weeks."

"I can come there then. For lunch? How about today?"

"Today?" I practically choked on the word as it left my mouth.

"Or tomorrow," he said.

He clearly wasn't going away. I glanced at my calendar and noted that I had forty-five minutes free this afternoon.

"Ben, I have thirty minutes free today at one, and that's it. Come here, and get this over with, or stop calling me. I'll leave your name with security."

"I'll see you at one," he said before ending the call between us.

I stared at my computer, not having any idea what Ben would want to talk about after all this time. Obviously running into me that night had shifted something in him that it hadn't done to me. Then again, he was male, and males tended not to really deal with issues right away—at least not in the same respect that females did. We would process things and deal with them immediately before moving on. Guys would only handle their emotions once they were forced to.

Seeing Kate's name on my call log, I considered calling her for a brief moment, but I decided to wait until after my lunch with Ben. Maybe he would have some insight as to why she was calling me after all this time. *What the hell was it about this family?* One chance encounter after eight years, and they were suddenly blowing up my phone like we were old friends.

My cell phone vibrated inside my purse, and I reached down for it, noting another text from Daniel.

> *I hope you're having a great day. I can't stop thinking about you. It's fucking horrible. What have you done to me?*

I smiled softly before turning off all notifications and setting the phone on top of my desk. Everything he did distracted me. Instead of reading the rest of the script sitting on my desk, all I wanted to do was pick up the phone and hear his voice. It seemed his face filled my mind every time my eyes were open.

It was official. Daniel had ruined me. I had to make it stop.

Between Daniel wrecking my life and waiting for Ben to arrive, I was so twisted up with anxiety that I thought I might fall apart. I wanted to get whatever this was with Ben over with, so I could go back to focusing on work, if that were possible anymore.

"Elizabeth? Ben is downstairs at security." Barbara's voice filled my office.

"I'm on my way. I'll be back before my call with Vancouver."

"Sounds good. Call me if you need a rescue." She looked at me, her face serious.

I found Ben waiting by the security podium with his hands in his pockets. His face lit up when he caught sight of me, and I wanted to punch him in the stomach for it. He'd lost the right to light up for me when he went down on my roommate, Kim.

"Thanks for seeing me." He smiled and moved to give me a hug.

I slowly backed away and shook my head, and he tucked his hands back in his pockets.

"You didn't really give me a choice. My assistant says you've been calling like crazy. What the hell do you want, Ben?"

Eight years of absolute radio silence, and now, he won't go away. *Not a single word spoken since that day in my living room, but now, he's standing in front of me at my work as if we were old friends.*

"Let's go somewhere to sit first." His eyes pleaded with mine.

I started to walk us in the direction of the studio commissary where everyone ate.

Once inside, I grabbed a tray and filled it with food. Ben followed my lead, filling his own tray with a premade sandwich, chips, cookies, and soda, before paying at the register. I led us toward a private dining area that I knew would be mostly vacant. The fact that we were at my place of employment irritated me enough. In case Ben caused some sort of scene, I didn't want any witnesses.

Opening the heavy wooden doors, I breathed out in relief at the empty space and chose a table near the back of the room. Sitting down, I glanced at the clock on my cell phone, knowing time was running out.

"So, what's up?" I asked between bites of salad.

"I miss you," were the first words out of his mouth.

I almost fucking choked. "You miss me? Are you high?"

His hand reached across the table, and I glared at it as I briefly considered stabbing it with my fork before moving my annoyed gaze to his face.

He pulled his hand back. "I know I have no right to you anymore, but seeing you the other night brought back all these feelings and emotions. I never got over you, Elizabeth."

"You sure seemed to get over me just fine," I sneered.

"How would you know?"

His face softened, and for a brief moment, I actually considered that he believed his words.

"We haven't spoken a single word in over eight years, Ben! Eight fucking years! I'm pretty sure you've been perfectly over me."

"You're mad," he countered.

I gagged. "You're insane."

"Are you over me?"

"Are you serious right now?" My eyes widened with my surprise.

"As a heart attack."

I wanted to vomit all over his plate when he said those stupid words. He used to say that line all the time in college, and I'd hated it then. Of course he still used it now.

"Ben, I've been over you forever. You and I happened a lifetime ago. I don't even know that girl anymore."

"That's not what I've heard."

"What the fuck are you even talking about?" I bristled as my anger started to rise.

"I've heard you never got over what I did to you."

I leaned forward, my elbows resting firmly on the table. "I got over what you did to me years ago. Do you hear me? Is it registering?" I knocked my knuckles against his skull.

"But I heard that I totally fucked you up, that I ruined you."

A strangled laugh escaped my lips. "I'm sorry, but no, you didn't. It wasn't about you or what you did or the fact that you cheated on me, fucked my roommate, or any of that. I got over all those things way quicker than I'd anticipated. The only

145

thing that stayed with me were your words. It wasn't even that it was you who had said them. It was just the fact that they had been said at all. They'd definitely affected me, but as you can see, I'm doing all right in spite of them." I forced a tight-lipped smile.

"You certainly are. I'm really proud of you, Elizabeth."

"No. I don't need you to be proud of me. You don't get to be proud of me. It feels like you're somehow taking credit for what I've accomplished, and I refuse to give you that."

He leaned back and ran his fingers through his thinning hair. "I didn't mean it like that. Shit. I just wanted to tell you how sorry I am for everything that happened in the past."

"Listen, Ben, I needed that apology eight years ago, but I don't need it anymore. Like you said, it's in the past."

"I don't think it is for me."

"What are you trying to say?" I asked, truly wondering what the hell he was getting at as my appetite all but disappeared.

He blew out a long breath. "I don't have closure."

"You don't have closure? For what?" I shook my head as confusion spread through me.

"For us. We don't have closure."

"Oh." I paused. "Seriously? You suddenly need closure? I'm closed. We're closed. We have the most closure you can have. It's called you-cheated-on-me-by-screwing-my-roommate-on-the-kitchen-table kind of closure. It's very specific."

"I'm sorry. I just didn't think. I mean…" He stumbled on his thoughts. "I've thought about you so many times over the years, and I wanted to reach out to you, but I never knew what to say. Then, seeing you the other night with Daniel and seeing how great you look—"

I put up a hand. "You don't have to do this, okay? We have a history and a past, and it was the first time seeing each other since everything had happened. I guess it's understandable that some sort of residual feelings might still be there, but you really need to move on."

"Like you're doing with Daniel?"

"That's none of your business."

"You're right."

"Speaking of though"—I took a drink of my iced tea—"do you know why your sister is calling me?"

His face twisted as his eyebrows pinched together. "Kate's calling you?"

"Apparently."

"It's gotta be about Daniel." His hand moved to cover his mouth.

"I figured as much. Any idea what about exactly?"

"Honestly? No."

"I should tell you one more thing"—he looked me in the eyes—"while I'm being completely honest."

"What?" I asked, having no idea what else he could possibly need to tell me.

"It wasn't an accident that I ran into you guys that night."

"What do you mean?"

"I've been trying to get Daniel to invest in something that I've been working on with my associates. He turned it down, but I wanted to try to convince him to give it another shot. I found out where he was having dinner and waited for him to come out."

I stared at Ben's face, and I knew he was telling the truth. Ben must have been the person Daniel had told me about that night he was upset outside my apartment. It made perfect sense that Ben wouldn't be the type to listen. His arrogance had always been his downfall.

While I was lost in my thoughts, Ben continued, "I had no idea he was with you though. I promise. And once I saw you two together, I forgot about why I was there in the first place."

"You're not going to ask me to talk to Daniel for you, are you?" I said with a slight grin.

"The thought had crossed my mind," he admitted.

"You know I won't do that. If Daniel said no, I'm sure there was a good reason. He's not an idiot, especially when it comes to good investments."

I couldn't help but smile. I found it ironic that, all those years ago, Ben had chastised me for being too driven and invested in my future, but here he was, trying to convince me that he was worthy of the same thing—being invested in.

Glancing at my phone again, I noted the time. "Ben, I've gotta get going. I have a meeting. We're done here, right? This is done? No more phone calls?"

He lowered his head and nodded. "Yeah, we're done here. I really am sorry for being such a jackass back in college. The things I said to you were wrong."

"I appreciate the apology. Thank you." I smiled, and for the first time when it came to Ben, it felt genuine.

Elizabeth

Barbara met me in the hallway, and I glanced down at my still silenced phone. Another text message from Daniel had appeared during lunch with Ben, but I hadn't read it until now.

> *You're not ignoring me again, are you? You know how well that worked the first time. Call me when you get a chance. I'm not desperate, I swear. Okay, maybe i'm a little desperate.*

Knowing that Daniel tended to do rash things, like show up at my office unannounced, I decided it would be in my best interest to send him a quick text message, so he wouldn't do something crazy, like come down here. The last thing I needed today was for Daniel to be here once this screwed up workday ended. I mentally noted how differently I had felt about him mere hours ago.

> *I'm slammed with meetings all day. Won't be out of here before seven. Call you then.*

As I turned off my screen, Barbara whispered, "Kate called again. She says it's important that she speak with you sometime today. To be honest, she sounds fucking nuts."

I sucked in a breath as we entered my office. "What the hell? If she calls again, just tell her I'm in a meeting until six, and I'll call her after."

She nodded. "I will. How was lunch with Ben?"

"Idiotic and overdramatic." I gave her a quick glance before grabbing a folder from my desk.

"Bob wants to take the Vancouver call in his office," she directed.

I nodded. "Sounds good. See you in about an hour."

The call with Vancouver had gone well, and I'd forced myself to remain focused by taking notes I didn't need. I'd had all the location scouting and stage information already, but I'd needed to concentrate to ensure that my mind wouldn't drift away to thoughts of Daniel. What had happened this morning could never happen again—ever.

After sending Barbara home for the night, I closed my office door and stared at Kate's number. I guessed the only way to figure out just what she wanted was to call her and ask, just like I'd done with her brother earlier.

The phone rang three times before Kate answered. "Hello?" She sounded out of breath and barely audible.

"Hey, Kate, it's Elizabeth." My tone reeked of confusion and unknowing.

She started crying at the sound of my voice. "Hi, Elizabeth." Her voice shook. "It's been a long time." She sniffed and sucked in a few shaky breaths.

Good Lord, what have I gotten myself into?

"What's going on, Kate? Are you okay?"

"No. No, I'm not okay. I'm not okay at all."

I threw my head back and pinched the bridge of my nose. I did not have time for whatever theatrics were about to occur. Bracing myself, I asked the million-dollar question, "Kate, are you going to tell me what's wrong, or do I have to guess?"

"It's Daniel." She sobbed into the receiver.

"What about him?"

"You can't have him, Elizabeth. I love him. I've been in love with him for years. Then, he meets you, and he just up and dumps me." Her voice rattled as her excitement grew. "No warning, no nothing. I hadn't seen it coming at all. One day, we were together, and the next, he never wanted to see me again."

Holding my breath, I waited for her thoughts to finish. When I was fairly certain she was done, I almost didn't know how to respond. On one hand, I felt awful that Kate was hurting, but on the other, I didn't owe her a damn thing.

"Are you there, Elizabeth? Did you hear me?"

"I heard you. I just don't know what you expect me to say," I replied honestly.

She sniffed again. "I don't know either. I guess I just assumed since we used to be friends that you would care more about my feelings, but that was probably stupid and naive of me."

"It wasn't stupid," I breathed out, not necessarily believing my choice of words.

We had barely been friends. She was the little sister of my then boyfriend, and since we'd lived on campus at our college, it wasn't like I'd spent that much time with her or even seen her that often. Then again, it wasn't as if I hadn't considered her a friend at the time.

"Then, you'll do it?" she asked, her tone sounding more upbeat than it had just two seconds prior.

"Do what exactly?" I had zero clue as to what she was referring to.

"Stop seeing Daniel. You'll break up with him?"

"Uh…" I paused, unsure of how to respond.

"You won't. You don't care about how I feel. I can't eat. I can't sleep. I haven't been able to function since he left me," she wailed.

I squeezed my eyes closed with the sheer force of the drama, wishing this were all a bad dream. I reopened my eyes and blinked, but I wasn't in my comfortable bed at home. Cradling the phone between my ear and shoulder with Kate's crying echoing into it, I realized this was a nightmare I couldn't wake up from.

"Kate, look, I'm really sorry that you're hurting, but I don't see how this has anything to do with me."

"You're joking, right? This has everything to do with you! Everything!" she screamed.

I wondered how the fuck Daniel had ever put up with this crap—let alone, how I'd gotten somehow involved in it.

"This is something you should be talking to Daniel about, not me."

"He won't take my calls. He refuses to speak to me!"

"I don't know what you want me to say."

"Get him to talk to me! Please? Tell him to hear me out. He owes me at least that much. I wasted two years of my life, for Christ's sake!"

"I'm really not comfortable with that. Like I said, I'm sorry you're hurting, but this isn't my problem." My head started to ache.

"Don't you have a heart? I know you do. I realize that it's been a long time, but I know what kind of person you once were. You used to care about other people, Elizabeth and I'm sure you still do. The old you wouldn't want to see me hurting like this. You'd want to fix it. I refuse to believe that you've changed that drastically," she stopped speaking and I stayed silent, listening to the sound of her breathing before she started up again. "I know my brother hurt you. You didn't deserve it, but neither do I. I know you can relate to how betrayed I'm feeling."

The idea of her comparing whatever she'd had with Daniel to my relationship with her brother caused me to bristle in my chair. "You're right about a lot of things, but I don't think that your situation with Daniel was anything like my situation with Ben."

"Maybe not exactly, but I was still invested in what we had, and I love him. I love him, Elizabeth. Can you say the same? Do you love him?"

I shrank back in response to her question, not that she could see it. *Did I love Daniel? No, not yet, but I knew the potential was there.*

"Do you love him like I love him?" she asked again.

"That's not really your business," I said with little conviction.

"If you don't love him, if you really don't love him the way I love him, then please let him go. Please send him back to me. I'm begging you, Elizabeth. I just need to talk to him, so he can see…"

She started sobbing again into the phone, and my heart softened as I heard her genuine pain and longing for a man who would never love her back. Her pain started to weigh heavily on me, and I had to break our connection before I caved.

"I wish you the best, Kate. I truly do. But please don't call my place of employment for things like this in the future. It isn't appropriate. You need to take this whole affair up with Daniel and leave me out of it. I do not want to be involved. Good night, and good luck." I ended the call without giving her a chance to say another word. My head was spinning, my resolve was breaking, and my heart was aching for the girl I used to know.

Daniel

"Daniel, Elizabeth Lyons is on line one for you." Serena's voice came through the speaker on my phone.

"Thank you. I'll take it. And, Serena? Go home," I responded before pressing down the button for line one.

"Babe!" My voice came out overly excited and I wanted to smack myself. *This woman turned me into a child.*

"I wasn't sure you'd still be at the office." She sounded off, and my stomach fell to the floor with the innate knowledge.

"You okay? What's the matter?"

I waited as she inhaled a single breath. My knees started to bounce under my desk as I feared what was about to spill from her lips—the lips that I had kissed, tasted, and loved just this morning.

"I've just had a really long and weird day." Her tone was riddled with avoidance and distance—two things I wanted least of all from her.

"What else? Something's on your mind. I can sense it."

"I just needed to tell you that I have a production deadline, and I'm not going to be available for the next few weeks."

"What does that mean? I can't see you for a few weeks? That's okay, babe. We'll have lots of phone sex," I said with a laugh, hoping to lighten the mood.

She didn't laugh back.

"I just can't have you coming down here unannounced and stuff while I have this big project on the line, okay? Promise me that you won't show up here without my permission." Her voice pleaded and she sounded desperate and nervous.

"Elizabeth," I all but begged, "what's really going on?"

I almost booked the plane in those moments where she remained silent. I hated the fact that I couldn't see her face, or look into her eyes, when I knew something wasn't right.

"I had a shitty day, okay? I got in trouble during my first meeting. Ben came to see me for lunch, and then Kate wouldn't stop calling my office."

"Wait. Slow down." I almost coughed on my words. "You got in trouble? What happened?"

"I don't want to talk about it."

"Okay. Tell me about Ben then." I tried to pull any information from her that she would give me.

"He tried to tell me that he needed closure between us. It was stupid, time-consuming, and ridiculous, but I'm pretty sure he's over it. I think he just needed to get some stuff off his chest after running into me the other night. It's no big deal."

I started fuming at the idea of Ben being able to see her when I wasn't around. I hated that he could be there when I couldn't be. It burned me to no end. "He came to the studio?"

"For lunch. It was fine. Thirty minutes was all the time I gave him," she announced sternly.

I huffed out an irritated breath. "Fine. What's this shit about Kate? Why was she calling you?"

"Exactly, Daniel."

"Exactly what?" I asked, slightly confused.

"Why the fuck is your ex-girlfriend, or whatever the hell she is, calling me at my office over and over again?" Her voice was laced with venom, and I couldn't stand knowing that it was directed at me.

"I have no idea. What did she say?"

A disgusted laugh filtered through the phone line. "She actually asked me to stop seeing you. Said she couldn't handle you breaking up with her. You won't talk to her, and she's desperate to talk to you. I don't know, Daniel. She was hysterically crying during the whole phone call, talking about how she is so in love with you."

I pulled at my hair as anger ripped through me. Kate had always been the mellow and laid-back type until I'd told her that it was over. She'd flipped her fucking lid that night, and she hadn't been the same since. I'd blocked her number from my cell and instructed Serena not to put any calls from her through at the office.

"I'm so sorry, Elizabeth. I had no idea that she would behave like that. What do you want me to do?"

"What do I want you to do? What I want you to do is not have girls who are in love with you call me at my fucking job, Daniel! I don't need this."

"I'll put an end to it."

"It's too late. It already happened. I didn't have to deal with any of this crap until you came along. I can't have this kind of stuff around me. I can't. I won't." Her voice was firm, and I could sense her mind solidifying its stance.

I'd known I might have to deal with this from her, but I hadn't thought it would be so soon. A woman like Elizabeth needed baby steps when it came to relationships. Even though we'd talked about it, things between us had been rushed. It was hard to stop something that felt this right.

"Don't do this, Elizabeth. I know what you're about to do. Don't do it."

"I need you to stay away from me, please. I need you to just leave me alone because I don't know how to balance whatever this is and my job right now. I'm absolutely overwhelmed with everything I feel for you. I can't lose focus, and you make me lose focus."

I could hear it in her voice that it was too late. She'd already decided.

"Please don't do this. I'm begging you not to do this."

"It's done."

She breathed out a breath as I lost mine.

"We'll work through finding the balance together. You think all these feelings aren't new to me? I've never felt this way about anyone. You're all I fucking think about all day long. That's normal, Elizabeth!" I desperately tried to convince her. "It's natural to feel like this when you're crazy about someone."

"Well, it's not natural for me. I don't like it. I feel out of control. I can't be out of control when it comes to this."

"Elizabeth," I mumbled under my breath.

"Just let me go, Daniel. Pretend I never entered your life."

"I could never do that." I refused to lie to her. "Could you?"

She sniffed, and I half-wondered if she was crying. It would tear me apart if she was.

"I don't know, but I have to try."

"I don't want this. I want to be perfectly fucking clear that this is not what I want. But if it's what you need, then I'll do it. I can't make you want to be with me." I admitted defeat, knowing that trying to change a strong woman's mind was like trying to reason with a drunk person. There would be no reasoning tonight.

"Wanting to be with you isn't the problem."

"Then, what is?"

"It's everything else that comes with it. It's too much for me. I'm not equipped to deal with all the extra crap. I want you—minus the crap."

I believed her because I knew, in this moment, that she believed the words herself.

"I wish you felt differently." *God, how I wished that more than anything else in the world right now.*

"I'm sorry. I don't. I just don't know how to do this."

"Good-bye, Elizabeth." I ended the call, knowing that if I heard her tell me good-bye, I'd fucking lose it. It was one thing for me to say it because I knew I didn't mean it. But hearing it from her lips, I knew she would have meant it, and that would have absolutely broken me the fuck apart.

Daniel

After driving over to Kate's shitty apartment, I let myself into her building and pounded on her door, half-tempted to knock it the fuck down. When it opened and she saw me standing there, her face lit up like she'd hit the lottery.

"Daniel," she breathed out and wiped her tear-stained face.

I pushed past her, walking into her living room before sitting down. "What the fuck is going on with you, Kate? Why are you acting like this?"

She started spouting off at the mouth, "Did Elizabeth call you? Did she tell you to come see me?" She moved next to me on the couch. "I knew she would. She's such a good person, but she doesn't love you like I love you."

The second Elizabeth's name had left her lips, I wanted her to stop talking.

I stood up and started pacing. "First of all, how dare you call Elizabeth at her work. Her work, Kate! Second, calling her and talking to her about us...who does that? Do you not realize how crazy that is?"

Her head lowered into her hands as her shoulders began to shake. I hated seeing women cry.

"I just wanted to get her to break up with you, so you'd give me another chance."

"You asked her to break up with me?" Her words spun around like a carnival ride inside my brain. *How had this become my life?* It was no wonder Elizabeth couldn't handle this shit. I could barely handle it, and it was my own doing.

"I just wanted to see you again, but you wouldn't talk to me." Tears continued to spill down her cheeks as conflicted emotions raced within me. "You ignored all my calls. I just wanted to talk to you, Daniel. I need to know why. What did I do wrong?"

Sitting back down next to her on the couch, I pulled her against my chest and let her cry. "Kate?" I said her name softly, knowing that only expressing my anger wouldn't solve anything. "Kate, look at me."

I reached for her chin and tilted her face up. She batted her big doe eyes at me.

"I never lied to you, did I?"

She wiped at her face before shaking her head.

"From the very beginning, I told you what this was between us and what I wanted from you, did I not?"

"You did," she choked out.

"Then, why are we here right now? Why are we going through this? Why are you ruining the best relationship I've ever had?" It was a low blow, but it was the truth. Sometimes, the truth hurt, and I needed to be crystal clear in this moment.

"Because I figured you'd change your mind. When we first started out, I knew that you saw me as just a friend, but I assumed, after time went by and you got to know me better, that you'd develop real feelings for me."

I shook my head. "I told you that would never happen."

"I know," she agreed.

"You just didn't believe me?"

"I guess I hoped for different."

What the hell was it with women? Were they incapable of keeping things uncomplicated? Clearly, the answer here was no.

"I'm sorry that I hurt you, but I never lied to you. I never promised you a future, but I understand now how you could have wanted one." I had to admit that my actions had been less than gentlemanly and certainly not always considerate even though I had intended for them to be both by being so honest upfront.

"After being with you for so long, I guess I just thought we'd never end."

"To be honest, Kate, I had no idea that I'd meet someone like Elizabeth."

Elizabeth had changed everything. My whole world had shifted the moment I found her. She was the one person who had tilted my world on its axis just by being a part of it. That was how it'd felt when Elizabeth stepped into my life. It wasn't something I could control or talk myself out of. It was just one of those things where a part of me had been drawn to her in that unexplainable way. People would talk about experiencing that kind of thing all the time. I'd always thought it was bullshit until it happened to me.

"I want someone to feel that way about me. I think I always hoped it would be you."

Knowing that I'd caused this pain forced me to try to make it better. I could be a complete asshole but not to her, not right now. She'd given me everything I needed for two years without complaint.

I hugged her tighter against me, rubbing her shoulder to help bring her comfort. "And I know, without a doubt, that you will find that guy, Kate. I'm just not him. You deserve someone who puts you first and wants to be with you all the time, not just when he needs sex."

She laughed, and my heart lightened.

"I'm really sorry I called Elizabeth."

"I know." I squeezed her gently, letting her know I forgave her.

"Desperate women do crazy stuff," she said with another laugh.

"You can say that again." I moved her body away from mine, and I pushed up from the couch. "Come here." I extended my hand and pulled her up. I hugged her long and hard, knowing it would be the last time.

I whispered, "You are an amazing woman. Don't ever forget that, and don't sell yourself short because of what we had, okay? You're going to make some guy extremely lucky, and if he doesn't know it or doesn't treat you that way every single day, he isn't the right guy."

A smile spread across her face as my words sank in. "Thanks, Daniel. I'm really sorry again for all the drama I caused."

"I know."

"Do you want me to call her and apologize? I probably should."

I briefly glanced away before meeting her swollen eyes. "No. This is something I need to do on my own, but thank you."

Closing her apartment door behind me, I headed for home, wondering how the hell I was supposed to live my life without Elizabeth Lyons in it.

12
Elizabeth

After getting off the phone with Daniel, I hung my head in my hands and bawled my eyes out, thankful that the studio would be virtually empty by the time I left. I would be mortified if anyone in the office saw me like this.

My heart ached inside my chest with each breath I inhaled. Somewhere in me, I knew it was the right decision for my career to tell Daniel good-bye, but I hadn't planned on him accepting it so easily. I hated to admit how much that part hurt. I'd never considered that Daniel would walk away without a fight, even though that's exactly what I'd asked him to do.

I tried to accept the fact that all I needed was time when it came to getting over him. With enough of it, eventually, I would feel whole again. But I didn't know if I believed myself. Daniel Alexander had reopened emotions in me that had been closed for so long. I wasn't sure how to go through this experience without him here to guide me.

It had been ten minutes, and I already missed him desperately. That sentiment alone caused me to feel foolish.

I woke up the next morning, and I could still smell him on my pillow. Inhaling the scent of him only caused me further pain, so I tore the sheets from my bed and tossed them into the laundry basket. I'd never get over him if he constantly surrounded me.

This was going to be harder than I had ever anticipated. Grown-up emotions were so much more intense than college-aged ones.

How was I supposed to get over someone like Daniel?

While driving to the studio, I tried to convince myself that if I buried myself in enough work, he'd eventually fade away. But I knew that was a lie. A guy like Daniel could never fade into the background after he'd been in the foreground for any length of time.

Wiping at the tears that started to fall, I pulled myself together as I walked down the hallway toward my office. Barbara's face saddened as soon as she caught sight of me, and she hustled into my private space before closing the door behind her. This had become an all-too-familiar scene lately.

"Oh my gosh, what happened? Why are you crying? Did something happen with Daniel?" Her rapid-fire interrogation refused to quit.

I nodded my head instead of answering, afraid of how saying the words out loud might affect me.

"What happened?"

"I broke up with him," I admitted before swiping at my eyes to stop the tears.

"Why? Why on earth would you do that? Did he do something?"

I glared at her, willing my sadness to be replaced with anger or annoyance or anything. Anything would be better than feeling less than whole.

"Yes, he did something! He invaded my thoughts and made me have sexual fantasies about him during the meeting with Mr. Kline yesterday! I totally spaced out while he was presenting! I'm surprised it didn't come to drooling."

Barbara was doubled over, laughing, her dark hair spilling down around her knees. I wanted to smack the living crap out of her.

She leaned up slightly. "I'm sorry. I can't." She continued to laugh. "Oh God, Elizabeth, that's fucking hilarious."

"Hilarious, my ass! Mr. Kline called me out in front of the entire meeting. He asked me what I was thinking about that was so much more important than listening to him speak."

"Oh shit, it's too much." She laughed even harder, her eyes narrowing to a squint with the force. "What did you say to him? Did you tell him?"

"I lied through my teeth. Told him I was daydreaming about a book I'd started reading that I couldn't stop thinking about."

"Oh Lord, seriously, this is priceless."

"It's not. It's really not," I chastised her, my tone clearly irritated.

"Okay, okay." She tried to level her breathing out by taking long inhales and slow exhales. "So, you got pissed at Daniel for this?"

"Yes, among other things."

"Tell me again how that was his fault?" She flipped her hair off her shoulders and pinned me with her stare.

I tilted my head to the left and leaned the weight of it against my fingers. "It's his fault for making me feel so much for him. I got stupid when it came to him, and my work suffered. I don't know how to concentrate on both! Then, my conversation with Kate last night—"

"Wait! You ended up calling her? What did she want?"

"She cried the whole time on the phone with me, Barbara. It was horrible. She's completely in love with Daniel. She asked me to stop seeing him, so they could have another chance."

Her lips pressed tight into a straight line before she opened them. "Tell me right now, you did not break up with Daniel Alexander and his gorgeous face because some stupid girl he used to fuck is in love with him."

"Not *because* of her, no. To be honest, I didn't appreciate the bullshit being with him brought to my doorstep. Why do I have to deal with that crap? I don't have time for that kind of drama in my life."

"Elizabeth, everyone has baggage. Everyone. But some people are worth unpacking for—or at least helping with their carry-on luggage or something. Don't you think he's worth it?"

"I do, but I'm really overwhelmed, and I feel like a failure," I admitted, feeling weak and pathetic—two qualities I despised.

"I know, sweetie, but you're not a failure. You didn't do anything wrong. You and Daniel are in that honeymoon phase where you can't get enough of each other, but you shouldn't punish him, or yourself, for that. You should be celebrating the fact that you found that kind of feeling in someone as amazing as he is. Seriously, you're both so lucky."

"I hate when you're logical."

"You just hate when I'm right, which is always, so you must hate me a lot." She smiled, and I leaned toward her, needing a hug from my closest friend. "You need to call him and fix this. He'll understand."

Reaching for the phone, I dialed his office, but his secretary said he would be in meetings all afternoon. Defeated, I hung up the phone, wondering if I'd blown my chances with Daniel after all.

Daniel

I knew I'd promised Elizabeth that I would walk away and give her space, but fuck that. I would not live without this woman in my life, and I wouldn't let her get away that easily after only just finding her. I didn't care what she'd claimed to want.

She'd tilted my world on its axis, and I refused to act like that didn't mean anything. Dealing with Elizabeth meant finding a balance between not scaring her off and also not really giving her a choice. I knew I needed to walk the tightrope between being understanding and being demanding. If she wanted to run, I'd hold on even tighter. This girl would not be pushing me away anytime soon, and I'd help her work through her fears because I had some of my own.

After charming a young girl into letting me inside Elizabeth's building, I waited outside her front door with a bouquet that was a single rose lighter and an overnight bag. I was optimistically presumptuous. I had no idea how long I'd be waiting for her to get home from work, but it didn't matter. I'd wait for-fucking-ever. It was cliché and cheesy as shit but so true.

When the elevator doors opened, she stepped out, wearing a tight-fitting dark blue skirt and a light-blue shirt, with her blonde hair falling down to her breasts. I almost fell to my knees at the sight of her. She was so beautiful. The look on her face when she noticed me made my heart leap inside my chest. Elizabeth was surprised but not mad.

I watched as she dropped her purse to the ground and ran straight toward my arms. Allowing the roses to fall to the floor, I reached for her and lifted her off the ground, holding on tight, as I inhaled her scent.

"I'm so sorry," she breathed against my neck before finding my lips with hers.

Her tongue wasted no time in entering my mouth, and I instantly hardened. I cupped her ass with one hand while my other hand pulled her shirt free before stroking the length of her back. I wanted her.

Her head pulled back, and a smile appeared. "I shouldn't have said what I did last night. I was hurt, upset, and confused."

"I know," I said with confidence.

"I'm so glad you're here."

"Of course I'm here." I smirked at her. There was never any other option. There would be no other choices for me again.

"Let me get my stuff, and we'll go inside." She turned to pick up the contents of her spilled purse, and I watched her ass sway from side to side.

Once inside her place, I forced myself to have some control. I'd have my way with her after we sorted this out. I placed the roses on her kitchen counter, and she sniffed at them.

"They're beautiful. Thank you." She inspected them, finding the one red rose. "One red?" she asked, unsure of the meaning.

"I thought you might be getting tired of all the white roses."

She stepped toward me with purpose. Grabbing my tie, she pulled my body against hers. "Never. I'll never get tired of getting white roses from you."

I waved my hand toward her couch. "I'm having a hard time concentrating on anything but imagining you naked, Elizabeth, but we need to talk."

"Well, that's a first—a guy who wants to talk before screwing. Aren't you full of surprises?" she teased me and I squelched my desire to spank her for it.

"I talked to Kate," I started off, figuring I might as well lay all my cards on the table right away.

"When?" Her head cocked to the side, exposing her neck, and I shifted my position.

"Last night, I went over to her place. She was a mess, but I honestly think we got it sorted out."

"How? She sounded pretty torn up on the phone." Her eyes creased together, almost as if she were channeling Kate's pain as her own.

"She was at first, but we talked."

"Just talked?" she asked as disbelief filled her tone.

I scowled with her question. It was completely unjustifiable. Elizabeth just hadn't realized that yet.

"I'm never fucking anyone else again, Elizabeth. Don't you get that?"

Her eyes looked away as a slight smile formed.

I continued, "I made her see that I never lied to her or led her on." I paused before clenching my jaw. "At least not on purpose. I can see now how my actions might have led her to believe that we could have had a future even though my words never said as much."

"That was big of you," Elizabeth complimented me, and it filled me with a sense of pride.

"Anyway, I told her what she deserved when it came to a man and how she should never settle for someone like me, and she agreed. She realized that I would never love her because she knew I could never feel about her the way I feel about you."

Elizabeth gasped softly, and her breasts pressed tighter against her blouse. She slowly moved back. "How do you feel about me?"

I leaned toward her, my hands reaching for hers. "I'm fucking crazy about you. I refuse to live without you, and I'm not letting you push me away. We both have fears, but we're going to work through them together. I told you before that I wouldn't let you sacrifice your work for me, and I meant it. I never want to give you a reason to resent me or hate me. But you can't shut me out. Just because I don't live here doesn't mean that you get to run away from me or stop communicating with me. As you can tell, I'll just come down here and get you."

She laughed, and her whole face radiated like the sun. "I'm crazy about you, too, and that's what scares me. I had the most explicit fantasy during a meeting, and I got caught. That's why I was so pissed off."

"Wait—you had a fantasy about me?"

She bit her bottom lip. "Oh, yeah."

"Is that why you said you got in trouble?"

"Uh-huh." She nodded.

"Keep talking, but in a minute, tell me every single detail, so we can re-create it." My dick started to harden again, no matter how many times I'd mentally told it to calm down.

"It's hard for me to admit being scared of things. It makes me feel weak, and I don't like that. A woman in my position doesn't get to where she is by being weak. But falling in love with you makes me feel that way. It makes me feel vulnerable."

"You're falling in love with me?" My heart sped up as if I were running a marathon, beating in double-time against my chest and pounding so loud in my ears. I suddenly felt as if I were the girl in this relationship.

"I'm falling for you so hard and so fast," she declared.

"You're not alone in that. Please don't think that you're the only one feeling that way. At least that should give you some comfort, right?" I wanted to calm her fears, hating the fact that anything about me scared her at all.

She agreed with a nod. "It does make me feel better, but I'm still scared, and I hate it."

"So, we'll get through it. Be scared. I'll be here to make sure there's nothing to be scared of. I'm not going to let you fail. I'm not going to let you fall. You're going to keep being the incredible business woman that you are, and I'm going to be by your side for it all. I mean, I'll be by your side from San Francisco, but still." I laughed as her eyes watered.

"Barbara was right."

"Oh, yeah?" I scooted my body close to hers. "What about?"

"She said that we were both lucky to have found each other and that some people were worth unpacking baggage for."

"Babe, I'll buy you more suitcases and storage units for all your baggage. I don't even care. I want all of you and everything that comes with it."

14
Elizabeth

How the hell I ever deserved to find someone as amazing as Daniel was beyond me, but right now, in my living room, I didn't care about the *whys* of it all. I was too thrilled being in the *nows* of it.

"So, you forgive me?" In order to move on, I knew I needed to acknowledge that I had been wrong.

"Of course I forgive you. It might not always be easy, but I know it's going to be worth it." He sounded so damn confident.

"You're always so sure of yourself."

"I believe in us. But promise me something, going forward."

"What's that?"

"That you won't shut me out. I will chase you every single time you run from me, but one of these days, you have to stop wanting to run. I want you to *want* to stop running."

How was it that this man, so new to my life, seemed to know me so well?

"I want to stop running. I do. It's just easier for me, but it's not fair to you. I know I have to start thinking about your feelings now, too."

"Yes, you do. I'm very sensitive in case you haven't noticed." He pursed his lips together and made a silly face.

"Oh, yeah," I said, rolling my eyes. "Promise me that you won't get tired of dealing with my shit?"

"I probably will," he said with a yawn.

"Great," I said, only half-joking.

He reached for me and pulled my head into his lap. "I might get tired of your shit, but you could always make it up to me with a blow job."

"I heard those cure everything." I stared up at his handsome face.

"Speaking of"—he wiggled his eyebrows—"tell me about that fantasy."

I shot up from his lap and jumped to my feet. "How about I show you?" I teased as I started stripping off my clothes. Kicking off my heels, I took three more steps before letting my skirt fall to the floor. I stepped out of it, and took a few more steps as I unbuttoned my blouse, seductively, one button at a time. I dropped it in my bedroom, quickly followed by my bra.

Glancing behind me, I watched as Daniel picked up my discarded items before dropping them in one pile on my floor. I stepped out of my thong and turned on the shower.

"Please tell me this was worth getting in trouble over," he said with a sly grin.

"I'll let you know after the shower." I moved inside and watched as he undressed, adding his clothes to mine on the floor.

Daniel opened the shower door and walked in. His hands encircled my waist, and he turned me to face him just like I had imagined. He leaned forward and kissed my shoulder before moving to my neck. "Did I do this?"

"Something like that," I said before craning my neck to the side, giving him all of it.

"What about this? Did I do this?" he asked before moving down to my breasts.

Water ran down them and onto his lips.

I moaned in response as he pulled my nipple into his mouth and circled it with his tongue. His hand massaged my other breast, and he licked and sucked at me before switching sides.

Water drenched his face, and I leaned forward, licking it off his lips, before he disappeared again, burying his face in my other breast. As he tugged the nipple between his teeth, I pulled his hair, enjoying the brief shock waves going through my body. He wasted no time in dropping to his knees.

He looked up at me, his hazel eyes shining. "I bet this was part of the fantasy, wasn't it?"

I sucked my bottom lip into my mouth and pulled it between my teeth as his tongue entered me. My hips bucked against his face in response, and his grip on my waist tightened as he held me firmly in place. Staring down at his wet dark hair, I watched as he devoured me, his mouth eating me like we were at the dinner table. His tongue lapped at my wetness, both from the shower and from my own excitement.

"You taste so fucking good. I love it." He glanced up at me before diving back in.

I fisted his hair in one hand and pressed his head against me, not wanting him to stop, as each lick elicited more and more pleasure from me. His tongue moved at a fevered pace, licking and sucking, and my body started to quiver.

"Oh God, Daniel. Don't stop. Please don't fucking stop," I begged.

He continued, each strong stroke making my breathing increasingly erratic. Waves of heat and ecstasy ripped through me, causing my body to jerk in response. I pulled his head away, needing the reprieve, as I came down from my high.

"Did we get that far in your version?" he asked, his face smug.

"If we got that far, I'd probably be fired." I managed a laugh before dropping to my knees. "Your turn," I warned before grabbing his manhood with my hand.

"Elizabeth, you don't have to," he started to say.

I took him into my mouth.

"Nothing. Everything's great here," he said.

I had to stop myself from laughing.

I continued to take him farther and farther into my mouth with each stroke until I could not take him any deeper. The moans escaping from his mouth told me he liked what I was doing, and I loved the way it made me feel. Knowing that I was the one bringing him this kind of pleasure made me feel powerful. His hand tangled in my hair as he softly pulled me toward him. It wasn't a demanding tug like I'd heard about from other women, but it was more like he wanted to be involved somehow and couldn't resist touching me while I pleased him.

"That feels amazing. You're so good," he groaned.

I worked him in and out of my mouth. His hips started to thrust against me, taking care not to push too hard or too deep, and I knew he was on the brink of coming undone. My hand stroked him as my mouth sucked simultaneously, and his head dropped back, water spilling down all around his body.

"I'm gonna come, babe," he breathed out before pulling out of my mouth and emptying himself on the shower floor.

"You didn't have to do that," I tried to argue while part of me was thankful for the save.

"I wasn't sure what you preferred. One step at a time, right?" He smiled. "But that step was fucking incredible." He helped me to my feet. "You do know we're in a drought."

"I know. We'd better hurry up and get out of here." I tugged at my partially wet and tangled hair.

Daniel turned the bottles on my built-in shelving, so he could read them before grabbing the one labeled *Shampoo*. "Turn around. I got this," he directed.

I did as he'd said. His fingers massaged my head, working the soap into a lather from the roots all the way to the ends.

"That feels amazing." I wanted to pass out in his arms. Having someone else shampoo my hair was an exhilarating feeling, but having Daniel doing it bordered on erotic.

He led me back toward the falling water, my back pressed against his front, as the water spilled down between us. My head tilted into the spray as he continued to work his fingers through my hair to get all the shampoo out.

"Conditioner is better," he said, his voice mimicking Adam Sandler in *Billy Madison*.

I laughed. "It makes the hair shiny and smooth." I played along as he squeezed it into his palms. "Start at the ends, please."

"Really? The ends?"

"Mmhmm. My ends need it most, and too much conditioner on my scalp will make my hair greasy. Ick. Just start at the ends and work your way up."

"You're the expert." He kissed my neck before following my instructions.

"This is really nice, Daniel. Thank you." I leaned my weight against him.

"Anytime you want me to handle your naked body, I'm all in."

He finished rinsing out my hair, and we soaped each other, taking our time in certain places, before shutting off the water.

"I'm probably going to get fined for all that water," I started to say. "But it will be worth it." I reached for a towel and wrapped it around my body as I exited the bathroom.

"I'll pay for it," Daniel said, following me close.

"I don't need your money." I walked to my closet and looked through my clothes.

"Are we going out?" he asked from behind me.

I turned around to face him. "Do you remember when I told you there was somewhere I wanted to take you?"

He nodded. "I do."

"Let's go."

"Right now?"

"If you don't mind." I paused, knowing full well that he most likely never wanted to leave the bedroom.

He leaned forward, his lips meeting mine in a soft closed-mouth kiss. "I don't mind."

"Yay!" I clapped my hands together. "It's one of my most favorite places in Santa Monica. It's only been open for private tours until recently."

"We couldn't go on a private tour, Miss Lyons?" He grabbed my waist and moved my wet hair to the side, so he could kiss my neck.

I pulled my shoulder up against his face. "We could, but it was only during certain hours, and it wouldn't have worked. That doesn't matter. We're going tonight!"

"Do I need to dress up?" He looked down at his still naked body.

"Well, you need to dress in clothing, yes. But not fancy ones. Jeans are fine. Did you bring jeans in that little bag of yours? Do you even own jeans?" I asked, realizing that I'd never seen him in anything other than suits.

"I didn't bring any this time, but I will the next."

"I'll dress to match you. Show me what you brought." He pulled out a pair of black slacks and a light gray shirt. "Always with the depressing colors," I criticized. "Let me go dry my hair really quick. Beers are in the fridge."

"Are we actually leaving?" He smacked my ass as I led him out the front door. "Nice outfit." His eyes traveled from the top of my black well-fitted top to the bottom of my dark gray pencil skirt.

I drove Daniel to the oldest hotel in Santa Monica. We entered the art-deco building and headed past the front desk and down the stairs into the darkened basement area.

"Are you murdering me? We just got back together, and you're already looking to kill me?" he whispered as we walked down the narrow staircase.

"Just come on. You'll love it." I pulled his hand.

Once at the bottom of the staircase, I made a left and pushed through the swinging dark doors. A new world opened up to us, and the energy shifted.

"What is this place?" Daniel grinned as he looked around.

"Pretty cool, right?" I stepped into the room as the past surrounded me.

"Shit yeah. Was this a speakeasy?"

"It was! Although, prohibition ended the same year they built it, so they didn't need to utilize most of the secret doors and hatches for long."

I looked around at the barely lit room. Red puffy booths lined the dark wood-paneled walls. All original fixtures remained, except for the carpet, which had been replaced years prior.

"The backs of the booths are all original. They've never been replaced. Ever. Al Capone used to sit right over there." I pointed to the largest booth in the corner.

"In that one?" Daniel pointed at it, too.

"Yep. He needed to be able to see people coming in from every angle, and that was the only seat in the place that let him do that." I smiled at the idea of being in this bar during that time period.

"Sounds about right, being back against the wall with no one behind him. What a badass," he said, seemingly lost in this place.

A hostess appeared virtually out of thin air. "Sorry for the wait. Do you know where you'd like to sit?"

Daniel pointed at Al Capone's old table, and she grinned as if she knew he'd choose that one.

"Right this way."

"So, do you like it?" I asked as we walked, loving that he seemed to appreciate this spot as much as I did.

"I love it. I can't wait to see more of your favorite places," he commented before sliding into Al's old booth.

"And I can't wait to show you," I said as I slid in beside him.

My favorite destination in LA felt even more happy and my heart was full.

EPILOGUE
Elizabeth

Four Months Later

Today marked the beginning of a new chapter for Daniel and me.

Wrapping up production for the day, I couldn't wait to head home to what awaited me. Upon arrival, I noted that Daniel was already inside, seeing his car parked in one of our underground spaces.

Bypassing the elevator, I practically skipped up the stairs as excitement coursed through me. When I walked through the door, I noticed boxes everywhere and shit scattered all over the floor.

"Daniel?" I shouted, wondering where he was.

"In the bedroom!" he shouted back before meeting me in the hallway.

"Hi." I smiled like a kid in a candy store before leaning up on my tiptoes and planting a kiss on his waiting mouth.

"Hi yourself." He pulled away before leaning back in and pulling my bottom lip between his teeth. "You ready for this?"

"It's a little late for that question," I teased.

He glanced around at all his things covering my floor. "True. I've already grown attached to my new place."

"Your new place?" I swatted his shoulder.

He lifted me up and tossed me across his shoulder. "Our new place."

"It's only new to you," I said, hitting his ass with my hands.

"I brought you something." He flipped me back over and rested me on my feet, before pulling me into the bedroom where the most elaborate bouquet of multicolored roses sat in an oversized vase.

"Daniel, they're stunning! So many colors. How come?" I ran over to them and breathed in their scent. "Does this mean you want to see other people? You don't want to just see me anymore?" I giggled with a fake frown. I loved any chance I got to tease him, but honestly, I was a little confused at his flower choice.

"I'll always only see you, but you're so much more than just my white rose. You're all of them—every fucking color. There are so many sides to you, so many shades, and I love every single one."

"I love you." I threw my arms around his neck and kissed him deeply, passionately, and with all the love I had for him in my heart.

It had been four months since we started officially dating. My scare when it came to my feelings had ended as abruptly as it had started. Daniel had coaxed emotions out of me and constantly reassured me that we were on the same page, so I never felt alone. Eventually, I'd stopped worrying about how to balance everything, and it had all seemed to fall into place. Trusting him implicitly, I realized how little there was to worry about. Work would dominate my days while Daniel would dominate my nights.

In the beginning, our evenings had been filled with late-night phone calls and our days with the occasional text or email. Being in a long-distance relationship had worked well for us for a while, considering how busy we both were with our jobs.

But after about three months, we'd simply missed each other too much, and being apart more often than we were together had become something that wasn't fun anymore. As much as the distance was a convenience in certain aspects, like no one to upset when coming home late for dinner or having to spend a night in the office, it had definitely made other things more difficult, like wanting to come home and hug him after a shitty day at work or simply needing my best friend when I wanted him around. Sending each other picture messages had grown old when what I truly wanted was him by my side, seeing what I was seeing. Life was about the experience, and we'd been experiencing our lives apart. And it had sucked.

Moving down to Santa Monica had been Daniel's idea. I would never have suggested it because the subject was honestly far too touchy for me. I'd never even considered moving up to San Francisco even though I loved his place and the energy of the city during the handful of times I'd visited him. But in my defense, the entertainment industry only existed in Southern California, so moving didn't make sense for me professionally, and I refused to give up my career for anyone, even Daniel. So, when I wasn't willing to make the same sacrifice, I couldn't in good conscience ask him to move down here, no matter how badly I wished he would.

Daniel had decided that his work could be done from anywhere, so he'd called me one day and announced his plans to relocate. I'd almost flown up there that afternoon to start packing his things. His best friend, James, had started running the actual office, but I'd often wondered how long it would take for him to join us down here. I'd gotten the impression that James couldn't be left unsupervised for too long. To be honest, I thought he missed Daniel, which was a feeling I could completely relate to.

I wasn't sure what that meant for Daniel's current business, but I could tell he wasn't worried about it. When I'd asked him once what would happen to everyone he employed, he'd assured me that they would all get at least a year's worth salary if he closed the doors and that he would try to find them jobs elsewhere, if not with him in his new venture. It pleased me to no end to hear how well he treated his employees. Good character was important to me, and Daniel Alexander was filled with it.

He tugged at my side. "I need a break. Can we go for a walk?"

"Want to have a drink and watch the sun set?" I offered, knowing the perfect spot.

"Sounds perfect."

We walked hand in hand along the sandy concrete path splitting the buildings on the street from the actual beach. I watched as Daniel looked around at the brightly lit pier rides and back at the people doing tricks on the metal rings and bars that were bolted into the sand.

"Is it always like this? Guys flipping around on rings and climbing ropes for no reason."

I laughed. "No reason? How else can they show off those muscles if they don't randomly start climbing that rope or balance themselves between a set of metal rings?"

"They could go to a gym."

"Oh, they do. It's down the street—outside in Venice."

His eyes widened as he took in my words. "Muscle Beach, right?"

"Exactly. You're a regular already." I leaned my body against him as he continued to walk.

"Almost there. It's up ahead," I said.

"Is it a bar?" He craned his neck to see where I was looking.

"It's actually a hotel, but the bar is amazing. They have a large terrace overlooking the beach, and gorgeous fire features. You'll love it."

When the enormous gray-and-white building came into view, Daniel's whole face lit up with his smile. "Is this where we're going?"

I nodded, squeezing his hand a little tighter. "Isn't it beautiful?"

"It's like the perfect beach house. I mean, if you wanted to house, like, three hundred of your closest friends. Yeah, it's gorgeous."

I pointed to the level above the ground. "We're going up there to drink our cares away."

"Everything I care about is right here in my arms," he said before tenderly kissing my lips.

Once we were seated outdoors, we each had an ice-cold beer in one hand and a menu in the other.

Putting our menus down, he brought my hand to his lips. "I can't believe we live together." He winked.

"I can't believe I get to have my way with you anytime I want." I leaned my head against his shoulder.

"Check, please!" he yelled.

"We haven't even eaten yet!" I laughed.

"You're the one who brought up sex, not me! I can't be expected to think about food after that. I'm only so strong, Elizabeth."

"You need your energy, so eat some dinner, Mr. Alexander. We can work it all off later."

"You'll be the death of me, woman."

"And you'll like it." I smiled.

"I'll love it. I love you." He pressed a kiss to my temple.

"I love you, too."

I stared at him, feeling the fullness in my heart.

We looked out at the sun and watched it cast a magical orange-and-yellow glow across the dark blue water. Turning my head to look at Daniel as he stared out at the wonder before us, I felt so blessed and lucky that he hadn't backed down all the times I'd tried to push him away.

Before him, I hadn't realized that what I needed was a strong man who wouldn't listen to me when I said I wanted him to leave me alone. I'd needed a fighter, and Daniel Alexander was exactly that. He was my champion, and I belonged right here, by his side, forever.

ACKNOWLEDGMENTS

These are going to be short & sweet, like these episodes have been! First of all, I wanted to thank you, my awesome reader, for taking a chance on something new and fun. It was fun, wasn't it?! LOL. It was for me! :) I had a blast writing these characters in this way (serial form), and I hope that translated while you read their story. Your support in me means the world. The fact that you read the stories I write is a dream come true. I can never thank you enough.

I also wanted to say thank you to Jillian Dodd and Michelle Warren—two ladies who read all my stuff before anyone else and threaten my life if I don't fix certain things or make it better or tell them WHAT HAPPENS WITH DANIEL AND ELIZABETH RIGHT THIS INSTANT!!!!! You ladies are true gems. Thank you for caring.

Last but not least, thanks to my All-Stars. You ladies are the craziest Sterling readers around, and I freaking love you for it! Thank you for loving me. :)

ABOUT THE AUTHOR

Jenn Sterling is a Southern California native who loves writing stories from the heart. Every story she tells has pieces of her truth as well as her life experiences. She has her bachelor's degree in Radio/TV/Film and has worked in the entertainment industry the majority of her life.

Jenn loves hearing from her readers and can be found online at:

Blog & Website:

WWW.J-STERLING.COM

Twitter:

WWW.TWITTER.COM/REALJSTERLING

Facebook:

WWW.FACEBOOK.COM/THEREALJSTERLING

Instagram:

@ REALJSTERLING

ALSO BY J. STERLING

In Dreams
Chance Encounters

THE GAME SERIES:

The Perfect Game: Book One
The Game Changer: Book Two
The Sweetest Game: Book Three

THE CELEBRITY SERIES:

Seeing Stars
Breaking Stars (Coming Soon)

HEARTLESS, A SERIAL:

Episode 1
Episode 2
Episode 3

CPSIA information can be obtained at www.ICGtesting.com
Printed in the USA
LVOW08s0433160615

442542LV00006B/904/P

9 781502 936004